ON THE SHORES OF TREGALWEN

First Printed Edition, February 2019

Published by Draft Horse Publishing

Special thanks to Ali Slagowski of Slagowski Hair Design

978-0-9851831-7-2

ON THE SHORES OF TREGALWEN

A CORNISH ROMANCE PREQUEL NOVELLA

DEBORAH M. HATHAWAY

DRAFT HORSE
PUBLISHING

BOOKS BY DEBORAH M. HATHAWAY

A Cornish Romance Series

On the Shores of Tregalwen, a Prequel Novella

Behind the Light of Golowduyn, Book One

For the Lady of Lowena, Book Two

Near the Ruins of Penharrow, Book Three

In the Waves of Tristwick, Book Four (Pre-Order)

Book Five (Poppy Honeysett's Story), Coming Soon

Belles of Christmas Multi-Author Series

Nine Ladies Dancing, Book Four

On the Second Day of Christmas, Book Four

Seasons of Change Multi-Author Series

The Cottage by Coniston, Book Five

Sons of Somerset Multi-Author Series

Carving for Miss Coventry, Book One

Timeless Regency Collection

The Inns of Devonshire—The Coachman's Choice

For Marinda and Jordan—

From childhood friends to eternal companions.
Yours is a love that is true.

PRONUNCIATION GUIDE

Tregalwen – treh-GAWL-when
Golowduyn – goal-oh-DEW-in
Rudhek – RUE-thek
Pryvly – PRIV-lee
Tykki duw (butterfly) – tih-kee DEW

PROLOGUE

Cornwall, 1811

The sea shone brightly as the summer sun cast its final light over the waves and adjoining countryside. Pink and purple clouds swirled across the sky in wispy strokes, as if a painter had swiped his brush haphazardly on his canvas.

A cool wind sailed over the sea and headed in the direction of Tregalwen Beach, where a boy and girl raced their horses across the sand.

"You started before me, Thomas Causey!" fifteen-year-old Hannah Summerfield shouted as her friend passed the finishing mark—a large monolith in the water—moments before she did.

Thomas tightened his reins and laughed over his shoulder. "You always accuse me of such, Hannah. When will you accept defeat gracefully?"

With a heavy breath, she shook her head, slowing her horse to a canter. "I will finish first one day, I assure you. I will practice every day until I do."

Thomas grinned, turning toward her. "You will hardly have time for that in London, mixing with fine society, as you will be."

He mimicked sipping a cup of tea, his nose raised in the air, but Hannah's smile faded away.

"Oh, don't remind me," she groaned. "I don't want to go. I would much rather remain here in Cornwall."

With you, she thought, though she dared not admit as much out loud.

She turned her horse to face Thomas more fully. She was taller than he was, but only just, his boyish frame matching her own slight figure. However, the confident way he held his horse's reins, his free hand resting on his thigh, made him appear older than his seventeen years. That is, until his brown hair fluttered across his brow in an unruly wave.

Hannah unwittingly sighed as he smoothed the lock back with a swish of his hand. Thomas glanced at her, a gleam in his eyes.

"You are looking at me in that way of yours again, Hannah," he said.

She cleared her throat, tucking her own stray, blonde hair behind her ear. "In what way?"

"Like you admire me."

She wrinkled her nose to hide just how accurate his words were. "You flatter yourself, Thomas."

"Really?"

His knowing smile made her heart flutter. She *did* admire him. In truth, she loved him. And she was certain he felt the same in return.

How was she to endure their separation? Unable to see his hazel eyes shining whenever he looked at her, or his lips that always curved into a smile when he saw her? What would it be like to be kissed by those lips?

"What are you smiling about?" Thomas asked, breaking her concentration.

She blushed. "Not a thing."

He narrowed his eyes but said nothing more. "We ought to

return to Rudhek Manor. You were supposed to be home by sunset."

"Oh, no. Not yet," she protested, motioning to where the sun had almost disappeared within the water. "You see? It is still shining."

Thomas shook his head, though smile lines appeared near his eyes. "Your grandparents will scold you."

"They have never scolded me," she said with a flippant laugh, "as you well know."

"Well, if they do not, your mother certainly will."

Hannah's smile faltered. "She knows it is my last night with you. She will not mind me staying out a little while longer."

She hoped so, at least. Her mother *had* told her specifically to come home early that evening, as they were to begin their journey to London at dawn, but Hannah could not leave. Not yet.

Mother did not understand Hannah's desire to stay in Cornwall. Hannah's mother, Lady Beatrice, the Earl of Wixbury's daughter, had married Mr. Summerfield for love and soon moved to his Cornish estate, Rudhek Manor. Mother had hoped that her marriage would lead to fine balls and parties, the sort she had experienced as a young woman.

However, after only three years of marriage, Mr. Summerfield—a man who preferred the characters in his books over anyone in Society—passed away from a sudden illness, and Hannah's mother was left a widow. Longing for a more "stimulating social life than Cornwall could offer," Mother had then departed to London, leaving two-year-old Hannah in the care of her paternal grandparents.

"A child is not meant to be in London," Mother had often said during her annual visits to the manor, "and *I* am not meant to be in Cornwall."

However, with Hannah's sixteenth birthday fast approaching, Mother had returned to Cornwall with a distressing decision.

"I am bringing you to London at last, my dear," she had said to Hannah, "and we shall celebrate your coming out with a ball. You may protest now, but I know you will grow to love your life there, just as your father would have…eventually."

But Hannah had a difficult time believing her words.

As she thought again of leaving Cornwall, she sighed heavily, casting her eyes about her. The jagged, brown rocks jutted forth from the cliffside to the ocean, waves shimmering in the sun's waning light. Long, flowing grass followed the curves of the beach where footsteps and hoofprints were visible across the sand.

How could tall buildings and countless shops compare with moors and the seaside? And more importantly, how could interacting with the fine Society of London even come close to the joy she felt while in the company of Thomas Causey?

She observed him again as he patted his horse's neck, and she tilted her head to one side. "Will you write to me while I'm away?"

He glanced at her sidelong. "I hardly think your mother will allow us to correspond."

"I'm certain she will not prevent me from exchanging letters with a friend," Hannah replied, her brow furrowing.

Her words did not sound convincing, even to her own ears.

Hannah's grandparents had never expressed a single concern over her friendship with Thomas, but as the heir to only a small estate, Thomas did not reach Mother's high regard. Instead, she had expressed her desire for Hannah to marry a wealthy gentleman in London. With such intentions, Mother had never bothered with Thomas, dismissing him as inconsequential.

As such, though Hannah hoped to write Thomas, she feared she would not be allowed to do so.

Being in London was looking more unappealing by the moment.

Thomas urged his horse forward, stopping when his leg brushed up against Hannah's. Her pulse quickened at the touch.

"I suspect you'll hardly have time to write anyway," he said. "My father speaks often of his time there when he was a young gentleman. The balls, parties, and concerts."

Hannah leaned back in her sidesaddle, trying to maintain focus as her leg tingled from his touch. "That all sounds rather dull, doesn't it?"

"Anything sounds dull compared to racing horses across the beach." He nudged her playfully with his knee.

She nodded, her spirits sinking lower.

"I hope you will enjoy yourself while there, though," Thomas said. His eyes were soft as he stared out over the gray ocean. "Only, not so much that you will forget Cornwall…or me."

Hannah's heart ached at the look of worry in his eyes. She reached forth, resting a hand on his knee, and a warmth spread from her fingers to her chest.

"Even if I dance with well-dressed gentlemen or speak with all of the fine ladies of London, I will never forget you, Thomas Causey."

Their eyes met, unspoken feelings passing between them, and he raised her hand to his lips in a kiss.

"I'll see you home now," he said, releasing his hold of her. "Do you have an excuse ready?"

Hannah nodded, her head still spinning from the touch of his lips on her skin. "Yes. I'll blame my tardiness on my horse throwing a shoe."

"Again? That reason will not suffice for much longer. You must devise a better one while you are away."

"Very well," she said. "*If* you promise to ride with me to the ridge before we leave."

Thomas seemed to contemplate the distance. "All right, just beyond that ridge—"

"The *far* ridge," she said, pointing further south.

His eyes smiled. "Yes, the far ridge. Then we will ride for the manor."

"All right."

He turned his horse around and reached for her hand again, their fingers intertwined between them as they rode across the sand.

"And soon," he said, "you will return to Cornwall and seek me out the very moment you arrive."

"The very moment."

His thumb caressed her fingers. "And we shall ride again on the shores of Tregalwen."

Hannah smiled at the boy she had loved as long as she could remember and wondered how she was to endure a single moment without him by her side.

CHAPTER ONE

London, 1814

"I know of your distaste for dancing and balls, Miss Summerfield, so how are you faring this evening?"

Hannah smiled at the gentleman across from her in the set. "Having the right partner eases my burden."

She had said the words many times before, always recited for polite conversation. Only this time, she meant it. She enjoyed Frederick Hawkins and his ready smile. He was not nearly so polished as the other gentlemen in London. His nose was not directed toward the ceiling and his friendly manner extended to everyone, no matter the class, which was why she preferred him over the others.

"Well, I have something that will make your night even better than a superb dance partner," Mr. Hawkins said, his dark blue eyes shining. The steps of the dance brought them closer together, and he lowered his voice. "Mr. Burton's hair."

He motioned down the set to where a gentleman glided around a wide-eyed, flushed-faced young woman. His hair, parted on one side of his head and extending to the other, fluttered up and down as he danced with exaggerated movements.

"Oh, dear." Hannah grinned. The action felt foreign upon her lips. It had been quite a while since she had genuinely smiled.

Mr. Hawkins nodded, raising his eyebrows high. "It looks as if one of the pheasants he hunted has come back to life and now flaps upon his head."

Hannah stifled a laugh with a gloved hand to her lips. "Mr. Hawkins, our mothers would scold us for such talk."

"It is good we have already agreed to keep our wicked ways to ourselves, then."

They reached out to hold each other's hands, and he winked at her. Yes, Mr. Hawkins was a breath of fresh air in London.

But it was still not the air she longed to breathe.

Despite Mr. Hawkins's attempts to cheer her up by mimicking the pheasant-haired gentleman's actions, Hannah continued the memorized movements of the dance, feeling more mechanical than joyful.

Finally, the music ended, and after applauding the musicians, Mr. Hawkins led Hannah off the dance floor.

The large ball, hosted by Mr. Hawkins's widowed mother, teemed with couples, so they paused every few moments to weave around fine gowns and shining black shoes.

During Hannah's first ball, she had pushed and prodded to get through the room, but her mother had quickly corrected her.

"London is different from Cornwall, Hannah," Mother had said. "Impulsive behavior will not be tolerated. You must act with decorum at all times."

Hannah had done her best to conform, but even after three years in London, she still itched to race past the others.

Before long, she and Mr. Hawkins moved forward, and

they reached the edge of the ballroom where Mother stood, her brown eyes twinkling.

"You two seemed to be enjoying yourselves," she said with a bright smile. "Always a lovely sight, the two of you together. Such a fine partnership."

Hannah noted Mother exchanging a look with Mr. Hawkins. Suddenly, he dropped Hannah's hand. His smile disappeared, and his cheeks shaded red.

Hannah regarded him curiously, but he averted his gaze.

"Thank you for the dance, Miss Summerfield," he said, his lips stretched in a strained smile. "If you will excuse me."

He made to leave, but Hannah, knowing she would not dance with him again that evening, called after him. "Are we still to ride tomorrow, with your friends, the Strouds?"

"Yes, yes, of course. I will meet you after luncheon."

Hannah nodded, tilting her head to the side as she watched him back away. He bumped into a gentleman who then splashed lemonade upon the woman in front of him.

"My apologies, sir, miss," Mr. Hawkins mumbled before turning around and disappearing into the crowd.

"How very strange," Mother said.

Hannah turned to see a knowing look in Mother's eyes, and a strange heat crawled up the back of her neck. She opened her white lace fan with a flick of her wrist, creating a breeze beneath her chin that caused her ringlets to flutter about her temples.

"Feeling warm after the exertion of your dance, my dear?" Mother said with a small smile.

"Yes. Might we ask Mrs. Hawkins to open a door?"

Mother nodded, her gaze sweeping across the room. "In a moment. Did you greet the Hiltons yet this evening?"

With a restrained sigh, Hannah nodded. "Yes, I believe so."

"We must call upon them soon. We wouldn't wish them to

think we have forgotten them after meeting them at the concert."

"Of course, Mother."

"And what of Miss Jamison? She is beneath us, but we must show everyone the same degree of civility."

"Yes, Mother, I spoke with her, as well."

"Very good. Oh, and we mustn't forget the dinner party we have with the Coreys this week."

"No, Mother."

Hannah rolled her head back slightly to relieve the tightness in her neck. She knew the beads of sweat glistening on her brow would beget Mother's criticism, so she dipped her head slightly in hopes of drying the moisture.

When she glanced up, Mother's eyes were upon her.

"Oh, my dear," Mother said, reaching out to give Hannah's hand a surprisingly encouraging squeeze, "I know you do not like to socialize. Your father did not either. Of course, this flaw can be attributed to being brought up in the wild, Cornish countryside. I should never have allowed you to be raised by the same people, in the same uncivilized manner."

Hannah stifled a yawn. Her own opinion differed greatly from her mother's, but after three years in London, Hannah had learned that arguing was more tiresome than even the constant demands of London Society, so she remained silent.

"At any rate," Mother continued, "I'm certain I could have changed your father's ways had he only lived long enough for me to do so. Why, look at how you have changed under my tutelage." She gestured to Hannah's stance. "Your posture has improved vastly, your conversation is far more stimulating, and you hardly ever forget to wear your gloves now. I daresay a number of gentlemen have taken notice of you. One in particular comes to mind now."

Hannah hardly heard Mother's words. A small draft blew past her neck, but it was gone before she could comprehend the coolness. She eyed the couples walking past her with rosy cheeks and broad smiles, and she took a step back, attempting to gain more space around her.

She longed to be free of London, from the throngs of people she was forced to mingle with daily. She would gladly replace all of it with the peace she had once felt, listening to the sounds of the sea waves crashing, herring gulls crying above her as she rode along Tregalwen with a boy whose hazel eyes wrinkled as he smiled.

At the thought of Thomas, Hannah felt a heaviness press down on her. When she had first come to London, she had unexpectedly been allowed to write to her friend, but after a few months, his letters unexplainedly stopped.

"I assure you, Hannah," her grandmother had said during one of her visits to London, "with his father's death, Thomas's time has been taken up entirely with running his estate."

"It is clear, though, that he is trying to live his life without your friendship," Mother had added. "I should like to see you do the same. At any rate, it is hardly proper for you to be exchanging letters with a boy you are not engaged to anyway."

So Hannah had stopped writing to him, as well. Though she had been unable to put him fully from her mind, she doubted very much that she would ever see him again.

"Hannah? Hannah, did you hear me?"

Mother's voice pulled her from her thoughts. "Forgive me, Mother. I was—"

"You were thinking of Cornwall again, weren't you?" Mother pressed a hand to her chest, her eyebrows raised high with sorrow. "I do not understand why, after so long apart, you now wish to leave me. I can only assume it is because you despise me for leaving you when you were a child."

Hannah bit her lip. She found it difficult to commiserate with her mother's self-pity when Hannah had assured her many times that she had loved her childhood and did not blame Mother for leaving her in Cornwall. Nothing Hannah said ever seemed to make any difference.

"I do not despise you, Mother. I merely wish to see my grandparents again and…and the manor."

Mother's hand dropped to her side, and she narrowed her eyes. "Is that all?" She waited, but Hannah said nothing further. "Well, we have been through this before. I haven't the stamina to make the journey, and you certainly cannot go on your own." She took a step closer, lowering her voice. "We have already discussed the sorry state of your grandparents' finances. When you were a child, you were a burden they could hardly afford. How could you ask the same of them again?"

Hannah ducked her head. Mother was right. Hannah would be very ungrateful if their funds were drained further for her sake.

"I understand perfectly, Mother," she said.

"Come, come, Hannah," Mother said, raising Hannah's chin with a stiff finger. "Your life is not so bleak as you sometimes imagine it to be."

"Of course, Mother."

"As evidence, let us continue with our earlier conversation." Mother's smile returned. "As I said, Mr. Hawkins has been behaving very differently this evening. Have you noticed?"

Thomas's hazel eyes still in Hannah's mind were replaced with Mr. Hawkins's dark blue. "I don't believe so."

"For once, I am grateful for your inattentiveness, if only so I may tell you this now myself."

Hannah narrowed her eyes, leaning in as Mother, practically beaming, lowered her voice.

"I have it on good authority," Mother began, "why, from Mrs. Hawkins herself, that her son is very much in love with you."

Hannah froze, her fan suspended in midair. "Mr. Hawkins? In love with me? Surely not."

"Hush, Hannah," Mother scolded, lowering her voice further and glancing around to ensure their conversation remained unheard, despite the swarming ballroom. "I assure you, he is. He also means to propose, and soon. Mrs. Hawkins and I, of course, are thrilled with the prospect of a marriage taking place between the two of you."

"A marriage?" Hannah blanched. "No, I cannot marry him."

Mother's smile faded away, and Hannah bit her tongue. She knew better than to speak so candidly. Had she learned nothing about keeping her mother happy?

"You enjoy his company, do you not?" Mother asked.

"Of course, Mother. However, I—"

"And he is so very handsome."

"Yes, he is, but—"

"Then a marriage *is* possible."

Her words caused Hannah's head to spin. Hannah and Mr. Hawkins had become friends over the years, but she did not love him. And she was certain he did not love her. He had always been kind and respectful to her, but she had observed him treating every other woman in Town with the same regard. How did that mean he loved her?

"You are…quite certain?" Hannah asked.

"Oh, yes. Mrs. Hawkins has said so herself." Mother paused. "Why, Hannah, you seem surprised. Did you have no idea of his feelings?"

"No, not at all."

"How can this be so? I was certain you knew. Mrs. Hawkins has said herself that you have done much to encourage his love."

Hannah snapped her fan closed. How could she have encouraged his affection when she was completely unaware of his supposed attentions until that very moment? "I most certainly have not, Mother."

"Oh, Hannah," Mother began, thin wrinkle lines appearing on her forehead. "This is why I was hesitant to bring up the matter at all. Indeed, I have known for days now. As you know, Mrs. Hawkins and I have grown so close over the years, what with our shared heartbreak of losing our husbands. There is nothing that would please the both of us more than to see our own children make a wonderful match with one another. You both would then experience the joy we have not felt in so long."

Hannah waited to feel the familiar contrition, the guilt that always arose when Mother spoke of her hardships, but the heat from the dazzling chandeliers and the dozens of bodies crushing around her distracted Hannah so completely, she felt little sympathy.

Mother clasped Hannah's hand between hers. "My dear, I wish only for your happiness. It would do my poor heart good to see you live beyond the isolation of Cornwall, to finally forget the life you left behind and experience London fully, where true happiness exists."

Hannah listened in a daze, unable to speak as her throat tightened.

"You would make such a fine mistress of Dawnridge," Mother continued. "Mrs. Hawkins adores you, and I should like very much to have Mr. Hawkins for a son-in-law." She leaned forward with pleading eyes. "If you married him, our family would be whole again. Do you think such a union could be made, Hannah, to help heal our family? Do you think you could marry him?"

Hannah could hardly breathe. Mother's expectant gaze produced an answer within her, the words echoing around her in monotonous tones as she said them aloud. "Yes, perhaps I could."

"Oh, I am so very pleased!" Mother exclaimed, clapping

her hands beneath her chin. She paused, looking around her as if only just realizing they stood surrounded by others. "But now is hardly the time to speak of such matters, is it? I'm afraid my excitement has allowed me to become carried away. Let us speak more about it tomorrow in the privacy of our own home. Oh, Hannah, you have made me so very happy!"

She reached forward, embracing her so quickly Hannah did not have time to respond.

"Now, I shall speak with Mrs. Hawkins about opening a door. You appear even more flushed than before. I can imagine why, but you must try to cool yourself before the next dance is called."

She walked away, speaking to herself about the plans to be made and people to tell once the proposal had been set, but Hannah stopped listening, her stomach tossing from side to side.

The musicians tuned their instruments in loud, discordant sounds, the flamboyant laughter and conversation swirled in her ears, and her chest rose and fell with quick breaths.

"Excuse me, Miss Summerfield?"

Hannah turned toward a young man standing before her, an eager smile on his lips.

"I believe I have the pleasure of having the next dance with you," he said.

Dance? She could not dance.

"Forgive me, sir," she said, grasping her fan tightly between her fingers, "but I fear I am no longer dancing this evening. Do excuse me."

Hannah darted past him, running from the ballroom and past the bewildered looks of others until she reached the street outside where she paused to catch her breath.

Mother had no notion of the sacrifices Hannah had made to adapt and conform to London life. Hannah's determined, spontaneous nature had been sapped away and replaced with reserved repetition and a life void of peace. And now she was expected to marry without love? It was too much. Never had Hannah wanted more than to simply leave it all behind.

She moved toward the carriages with a determined step.

Peace. That was what she needed. Time away to think, to allow peace once more into her life.

And she knew exactly where to go to receive it.

CHAPTER TWO

Cornwall, 1814

Thomas Causey shook his head, averting his gaze from the dinner party invitation that lay open on his desk.

When would the mothers around St. Just stop attempting to marry their daughters off to him? Their unsuccessful efforts had become excessive ever since he had inherited Leighton House.

"Thankfully I have an actual excuse not to attend this one," he said aloud to the empty room.

The rest of his household had already retired, leaving him alone with a crackling fire in the hearth and rain sliding down the outside of the window in his study.

A candle cast its glow upon his desk, letters of business, lists of repairs needed at his tenants' homes, and more invitations from even more mothers scattered across the mahogany wood.

He scribbled out a quick decline to Mrs. Stedman, knowing he ought to have responded earlier than the day before the party.

I've been busy, he thought, *seeing to the affairs of the estate.*

His excuse was mostly true. He *had* been busy, no matter that it was all his own doing to keep his thoughts from straying to things, and people, he ought not dwell on. Not anymore.

After all, he had learned rather quickly that *she* did not think of him. When Hannah had lived in London for no longer than a year, Thomas had asked if he could visit her. To his dismay, Hannah gave no response to his request, and soon her letters had stopped altogether. He was eventually forced to consider that either Mother had finally convinced Hannah to embrace London and leave Cornwall behind…or Hannah had become attached to another, despite her grandparents claiming the opposite only days before.

In truth, Thomas found the fact that she remained single after three years in London shocking, for who could not love Hannah Summerfield? Even as a boy, he had loved her. She was adventurous, carefree, and enchanting with blue eyes that sparkled brighter than the sea at midday.

"But I should not think of her," he reminded himself, crossing the room to toss another log onto the dying embers in the hearth. "I shall not see her again."

A single flame lapped up the side of the log, and as he watched it dance in the air, he could not help but hope that perhaps one day he would be proven wrong.

Hannah regretted at once her impulsive decision to leave the stagecoach behind and complete the rest of her journey to Rudhek Manor on foot.

The driver had offered to take her farther down the lane, but as Hannah had been sitting near an ample-sized woman for nearly three hours, she had taken the very first opportunity to remove herself and her lady's maid from their tight quarters and freely explore the countryside around them.

That was her first mistake.

Her next was assuming she could still find the way to her grandparents' home. She had been certain it was just down the road, but as the sky grew darker, the rain fell harder, and the road grew longer, she wondered if she had become lost in the vast countryside after all.

At least I have the sense to remain on the road, she thought.

Though, which road she was on, she was no longer certain.

"Careless," she muttered to herself as she trudged through the mud, brown specks flinging higher and higher up her skirt with each step. "That is what I am. Absolutely careless."

"What was that, miss?"

Hannah looked over her shoulder to where her lady's maid walked behind her. Even in the darkness, Hannah could see the weariness in her eyes and the sinking of her shoulders.

"Oh, I was merely stating that…you ought to take heart, Daisy. I am certain we are almost there."

"Yes, miss."

Hannah smiled at her with an encouraging nod before facing forward.

Poor girl. She certainly did not share the same level of enthusiasm as Hannah when tramping through a storm in the darkness. If Hannah could have made the journey from London alone, she would not have had to drag the girl from her bed in the early hours of the morning without a word to anyone. Blasted Society and their rules of impropriety. And blasted mothers who inflicted their own desires upon their children.

Hannah grimaced. She knew she would not have received consent to go to Cornwall had she asked, just as she knew she would be pressured into truly marrying Mr. Hawkins if she remained in London. As such, she had no choice but to leave—as soon as she could manage *and* without her mother's knowledge.

Even as the August rain poured down in droves upon

them, Hannah found it very difficult to feel remorse for her actions. Her body had grown weary from three days of travel, but her spirits refused to dampen—unlike her bonnet and cloak that no longer kept the rain from her person—for she had finally arrived in Cornwall.

She longed to see the yellow gorse blooming along the road, the tors stacked high in piles of gray stone, and the waves rushing upon the sand, but the darkness prohibited any sight-seeing at all.

That is, until a few glowing lights appeared in the distance. Hannah smiled, hastening her step. "There, I remembered the way after all."

"Thank goodness," she heard Daisy mutter.

Hannah switched her large bag to her other hand. Stuffed inside was a spare dress, a change of underclothes, her shawl, and a few pairs of gloves, all she had been able to gather before her departure.

Her lack of belongings was the least of her concerns, however, as she splashed through the puddles, apprehensive to think of how her grandparents would react to her unexpected arrival.

"You were a burden," Mother had said, "a burden that they could hardly afford."

Hannah's stomach turned. She knew her grandparents would do anything for her. They always had. She flinched at the idea of further draining their waning finances, but what other choice did she have? She had no intention of returning to London, and the little money she had was expended on the coach and nightly rooms. Her only option was to tell her grandparents she was willing to earn her keep…and pray they were as generous as they always had been.

Hannah continued toward the lights of the Summerfields' manor, but when the characteristic hedge lining the road to her grandparent's estate did not appear, she frowned.

She wiped the rain from her eyes, squinting to better see into the distance. When she caught sight of a two-storied house, light from the windows revealing ivy that climbed up one side of the stone, her breath caught in her throat, and her feet stopped in their tracks.

"Leighton House?"

"What is it, miss?" Daisy asked as she came to stand beside her. "Is it not your grandparents' home?"

Hannah bit her lip, shaking her head. "No, it is not."

"Well, do you know whose house it is?"

She could hear the thinly veiled despair in Daisy's tone.

"It is…an old friend's."

"Perhaps she can help us reach your grandparents, as we seem to have lost our way."

Hannah didn't bother to clarify that her friend was a gentleman. The thought of Thomas sent her mind spinning. Would she still be welcome in his home after they had not spoken in years? And what would he think, her appearing at his doorstep unannounced in the dark, looking the way she did, after being gone for so long?

"No, I think we're better off going to Rudhek Manor ourselves," she said. "I know the way from here. I have made the journey before many times."

And she could do it again.

Ignoring the look of horror on Daisy's face, she turned around. The darkness that instantly enveloped her, however, made her pause once more.

What was she doing? The air had chilled, her limbs had begun to ache from the journey, and her stomach grumbled. She'd not had more than a slice of cold meat at the inn where they had stopped for dinner. It was a miracle she had not collapsed already in the middle of the road. And Daisy even more so.

No, it was time to be sensible and seek help at Leighton

House. Thomas would still consider her a friend. She was certain he would help her.

"Very well," she muttered, turning back to the small estate. "Let us seek help there."

She didn't miss the relief in Daisy's eyes.

Hannah pulled her feet out of the mud and moved forward with a raised chin.

I shall knock softly and allow the butler to see to me first, she sorted out in her mind as she kicked her skirts away from her legs. *Then I shall have a moment to compose myself before Thomas is even alerted.*

She moved up the small set of stairs to the front door before Daisy spoke behind her. "Shall I go around the back, miss?"

"No, don't be silly. You just stay with me. I'll see that we both get warmed."

Daisy took a few steps back, bowing her head. She was clearly uncomfortable not using the servant's entrance, but Hannah had too much on her mind to worry about Daisy's sense of propriety.

She reached up and rapped her knuckles against the wood. Trepidation filled her chest but also something akin to excitement bubbled just behind it.

Thomas. How she had missed him.

Footsteps sounded within the house, then the door clicked and opened.

"Forgive me," Hannah said. "I was headed for Rudhek Manor, but in the darkness, I somehow missed the turn. I would—"

"Hannah?"

Her eyes adjusted quickly, and the dim candlelight coming from within the home revealed a pair of hazel eyes she would know anywhere.

She had always imagined their reunion a little differently.

Perhaps in the daytime with a little less rain, definitely less mud. Still, seeing him produced a familiar stirring within her heart. Before she could think, she launched toward him and wrapped her arms around his neck.

"Hello, Thomas!"

CHAPTER THREE

Thomas stood frozen, blinking in stunned silence as Hannah, *his* Hannah, embraced him in the doorway of his home. He looked over her shoulder to see a girl, no doubt her lady's maid, standing nearby with a wide-eyed, averted gaze, looking no doubt as surprised as Thomas felt.

Was it truly Hannah embracing him? Had he conjured her from his thoughts only moments ago?

Her laughter in his ear, soft and lilting, jarred his senses, and only then did he realize his arms hung limply at his sides. He slid his hands around her, holding her close as a flood of emotions and memories rushed over him. Moisture began to seep through his shirt from her wet clothing, but he did not release his hold.

What was she doing here? Why did she send no notice of her coming? His mind was inundated with questions, so he pulled away to take in the sight of her, his fingers at her waist, her hands on his shoulders.

"Hannah, what are you…" He paused, staring at the mud smeared across her cheek and forehead, rain dripping from the ends of her blonde hair. Her dress was entirely drenched, her sodden bonnet lopsided, but he had never seen her more beautiful. Her round face had given way to a more slender shape, accentuating her high cheekbones and dimples, but her eyes still sparkled the same shade of blue.

"Oh, dear, I've made your shirt wet," she said with a sheepish grin. She patted his chest with her hand where the fabric clung to his skin.

Her touch produced a burning sensation in the center of his chest.

"That is no matter," he said, taking a step back and releasing his hold of her. "Please, come in. You must be frozen."

As if on cue, Hannah shivered, walking into the entryway and speaking over her shoulder. "Come along, Daisy. You mustn't be frightened of Mr. Causey here. He is as kind a gentleman as any. He and I are dear friends." She paused, looking over at him. "Aren't we?"

He couldn't understand the hesitance dimming her eyes. "We are, indeed."

Her uncertainty melted away, revealing a dazzling smile, and Thomas's head spun.

"You must forgive my intrusion," Hannah said next, her voice giving a jerking sound as she shivered again. "As I said, we left the stagecoach behind, and as it grew dark, I must have taken the road that led me here instead of to my grandparents' home."

"It is no trouble, of course," he responded. "There is a fire lit in the study. You remember the way."

She nodded, turning to the corridor on the right. He followed behind her, staring in amusement at the puddles of water she left behind with each step. His mouth continued to open and close, unable to settle on what to say, so rapidly did his mind churn through questions about her reappearance.

"So, you traveled by stagecoach?" he finally asked her.

"Yes, we did. I had forgotten how long and arduous the journey was."

They entered the study, and as Hannah pulled the hesitant Daisy toward the hearth, Thomas rang the servant's bell and retrieved a couple of blankets from a hutch near his desk.

"And your mother agreed to you traveling in such a way?"

Hannah paused in removing Daisy's bonnet and cloak. She looked over at Thomas, squinting her eyes in a sort of wince.

He chuckled. "She doesn't know you've come, does she?"

Hannah continued helping the girl before removing her own sopping outerwear. "We have traveled for nearly three days, so I hope she has noticed my absence by now."

Thomas took the clothing from Hannah and draped it over a chair, water pooling instantly beneath them, before he handed her the blankets.

"I assume you left a very vague note?"

Her dimples deepened as she wrapped the fur cover around Daisy. "The vaguest."

He smiled and watched her nearly force her lady's maid to sit near the fireplace. The girl was clearly uncomfortable with the attention Hannah showed her.

"And when did you decide to come to Cornwall?" he asked next.

Hannah straightened and turned to face him, throwing a blanket around her shoulders with a smile as vibrant as he remembered.

"About six hours before I left."

He couldn't help but laugh again. "You are still the same as you have always been, I see."

Slowly, her smile faded away. "Yes, still just as daft."

"No, not daft," he said at once, wondering at her self-deprecation. "I was merely saying you were still impulsive. And there is certainly nothing wrong with that, so long as you are happy."

She stared at him, her mouth parting. He wondered if he should tell her about the mud on her brow and cheek, but she looked even more appealing with the imperfections, so he remained silent.

Before they could say another word, the door opened, and he tore his gaze away from Hannah as the housekeeper entered the room with a nightcap on her head. When her eyes fell upon Hannah, the woman visibly stiffened before turning to Thomas with a curtsy.

"Sir?"

"Mrs. Parr, you remember Miss Summerfield?"

The housekeeper narrowed her eyes over her pinched nose. "Miss."

"Lovely to see you again," Hannah said with a blush before averting her gaze.

"Forgive my late-night request," Thomas said, "but would you mind calling for the carriage? Miss Summerfield and her lady's maid could also benefit from a cup of tea and a few biscuits, I think."

"Of course," Mrs. Parr said, and she turned on her heel and left the room, but not before sending a suspicious glance in Hannah's direction.

"I really do not wish to cause trouble," Hannah said as soon as they were alone.

Thomas shook his head, motioning to the chair nearby as he sat down upon the sofa across from her. "Nonsense. You spent half of your childhood within these walls, Hannah. Just because Mrs. Parr undoubtedly recalls the number of pies you stole from our kitchen does not mean you should feel uncomfortable here."

Hannah pressed a hand against her brow as she sat. "You think she remembers that, then?"

"Did you see the look she gave you as she left?" he asked with a quirked brow. "She absolutely remembers. And our cook does, as well."

"Oh, dear."

"I would not worry too much about it. After all, they have forgiven *me* for sharing in the spoils of your thievery."

Hannah scoffed. "Thievery. They were hardly jewels. And I only did so once or twice—"

"Every month. For fifteen years."

Hannah beamed at Thomas's teasing. Was she really there with him in his study, speaking like the old friends they were? She felt as if she were in a pleasant dream from which she never wished to be awakened.

She leaned back in her chair, considering him once more, still reeling at the changes that had come over him.

His boyish frame had nearly doubled in size, broad shoulders and a lean figure revealing that the gentleman was not afraid of working hard on his estate. He had grown a full head taller than Hannah, something she had been quick to realize when she had to stand on the tips of her toes to embrace him. His strong jaw was shadowed in stubble she was certain he had been unable to grow before, and his hair no longer fell across his brow. However, his grin, even after all those years, still caused her heart to flutter.

As the warmth from the fire soothed her limbs, Hannah leaned back in her chair with a smile. "How very strange this is, to be here with you as if no time has passed by at all. Has it truly been three years since we have seen one another?"

Thomas nodded. "And two since we last exchanged letters."

A heavy silence filled the room. Thomas had mentioned only moments ago that they were still friends, but did his lack of letters truly denote his desire to end further association with her? If so, she was an absolute fool for going to his house at all.

"So, tell me," Thomas said across from her, breaking

through the silence, "how was living in London? I gather you grew to love it after all?"

The dark cloud creeping over Hannah's spirits grew thicker. Images of bright chandeliers and swirling dancers replaced any peace that might have appeared upon her arrival in Cornwall.

"No," she began, "I did not care for it."

Thomas pulled back, a look of confusion settling on his brow before he nodded. "Just as you predicted, then?"

She forced a smile. "Just so."

"Your mother still enjoys it, though?"

Hannah fought a grimace. She did not want to think of the woman. That would mean acknowledging the fact that Hannah had agreed to consider marrying Mr. Hawkins. Should she go back on her word, she assumed Mother would threaten to strip her of her dowry, and with her grandparents' declining funds, Hannah was running out of options for a livable future.

Before her worrisome thoughts could continue further, Hannah took a deep breath and forced another smile.

"Yes, Mother enjoys London," she said, "but I still prefer Cornwall."

Thomas nodded. " I am glad to hear that."

The door opened again, and Mrs. Parr entered with a small tray, placing it rather noisily on the table before leaving the room with a bobbed curtsy.

"You are right," Hannah said, her brows pulling close together. "She does remember me."

Thomas laughed again, the deep, rich sound causing her to forget about the wet clothing still clinging to her body and the unpleasant thoughts of London.

"Did you make many friends while there?" Thomas asked, pouring the tea into two cups.

"I suppose."

She accepted the cup he offered her and watched as he

extended the second to Daisy. The maid took it with trembling fingers, staring down at the tea as if she had never drunk before.

"And how many gentlemen's hearts did you manage to break?"

The blood drained from her face, shots of alarm soaring throughout her body. Did he know about Mr. Hawkins? She was certain she had never written about him. There had been no reason to. Could Mother have told him though? Her grandparents?

"Why, none, I hope," she replied with a nervous laugh.

Thomas must have caught her discomfort. He nodded and looked away.

Hannah glanced to Daisy, who appeared entirely unaware of their conversation as she stared into the fire, blinking slowly with fatigue. Then Hannah returned her attention to Thomas. "Do you enjoy running Leighton House as your own?"

"I do. The work the estate provides me with is very satisfying."

She nodded, and an uncomfortable silence arose between them. She took a sip of her tea, the liquid spreading throughout her like a blazing fire.

What was the matter with her? She had not spoken face-to-face with Thomas in years. There ought to be hundreds of questions to ask him. So why could she think of nothing to say?

As images of white cravats, shined shoes, and dignified brows spun about her mind, she knew why. She wished to speak with Thomas just like before, but how could she after they had both changed and their relationship suffered?

Nothing was the same as before, and the realization caused a great sadness to press down on her mind.

"Do you know how long you are to stay?"

Thomas's voice rang in her ears. "No, I do not."

"Well, what with your hasty departure, I don't imagine

that you have had the opportunity to think much on what you will do while here."

"No, I haven't really."

He averted his gaze. "Do you recall the small gatherings we used to have on Tregalwen Beach? With the farmers, our tenants, and a few of our neighbors?"

Hannah's spirits lifted slightly at the pleasant memories his words evoked. "Of course. I always enjoyed them."

"Well, we are holding one tomorrow evening," he said, his fingers tapping upon his knees. "I understand if you wish to spend your time with your grandparents, though they are welcome to join us, as well, but do you think you might wish to come?"

Hannah's heart swelled. "I would love to, Thomas."

The creases around his eyes returned as he smiled. "Excellent."

Mrs. Parr entered the room then, drawing their attention to her lingering, tight-lipped expression. "The carriage is ready, sir."

"Thank you," Thomas said with a sidelong glance at Hannah.

"Yes, thank you for your trouble," Hannah said, setting her cup aside and standing from her chair. She made to say more, but when she followed the woman's disapproving gaze to the mark her wet gown had left upon the chair, she cringed. "Oh, I am terribly sorry."

Thomas merely smiled. "Not to worry, Miss Summerfield. It will dry. Will it not, Mrs. Parr?"

The housekeeper's nostrils flared as she gave a curt nod and left the room with a curtsy and a swish of her skirts.

Thomas's barely restrained laughter filled the room, and Hannah held a finger to her lips, though she laughed right alongside him as they left the study.

A short carriage ride later through the mud and rain, and Hannah, Daisy, and Thomas arrived at Rudhek Manor. The butler showed Daisy the way to the servant's quarters before he sought out Hannah's grandparents.

Hannah remained in the entryway, not wishing to track water throughout the manor like she had done at Leighton House. As her eyes roved over her childhood home, a feeling of nostalgia washed over her.

The third step on the carpeted staircase still held the stain where she had spilled hot chocolate, sneaking a cup to her room after dark. The floral curtains framing the leaded windows remained patched in the top corner—a sign of where Hannah had torn the fabric, swinging from it as a child.

A blush spread across her cheeks at the evidence of her burdensome, childish behavior, and she worried again over how her grandparents would react to her arrival.

She fleetingly noticed the new chandelier lighting the room and the fresh coat of blue paint upon the walls before her eyes fell upon Thomas, who remained near the door.

Suddenly, Hannah became acutely aware of their seclusion. She had not been alone with Thomas, or any gentleman for that matter, in three years. Ever since she had ridden on the beach with him.

"Will you wait for my grandparents to come down, so you may see them, as well?" she asked, her hands wringing together.

Thomas shook his head. "No, I'll leave you to enjoy your reunion with them alone."

"Of course." She stared at the floor. "I must thank you for your help this evening. Especially for not turning me back out into the rain when I appeared before you in such a way."

He nodded in silence, appearing to hesitate a moment before taking a step toward her. "Hannah, I am so pleased to see you again. I hope tomorrow we may speak more, like we used to."

Their eyes met, and her breath hitched when he reached forward, brushing a soft thumb against her cheek. "You may want to wash up a bit before then, though." And with a wink that caused her heart to flutter, he slipped through the door and left the manor before she could say a word.

Hannah raised a hand to her tingling cheek, and she blushed as she felt the mud caked to her skin.

Instead of cringing at what she must look like, she could only smile.

It was true they had both changed over the years, but perhaps not everything was so very different, after all.

CHAPTER FOUR

"I see you remembered where we kept the paint."

Hannah looked over her shoulder to see her grandmother, Mrs. Ann Summerfield, entering the parlor.

"Yes, Grandfather was kind enough to allow me the use of them," she replied. "I hope that is all right."

"Of course," Grandmother said, placing a kiss atop Hannah's head. "We have always kept up a fresh supply, hoping you would return to use them. And now, here you are."

Hannah smiled at her grandmother before looking back at her canvas. She sat facing the window, hoping to capture the view of the green countryside rolling beyond the manor, but her mind dwelled on her grandmother's eyes focused in her direction.

The previous evening, after their initial shock had faded, Hannah's grandparents had welcomed her to Rudhek Manor with open arms. Hannah had been foolish to think they would do otherwise, but she still sat uneasy that morning, for she did not relish the thought of asking her grandparents if they could afford to keep her.

"Did you sleep well, my dear?" her grandmother asked,

moving to sit on the nearby sofa. She leaned back, a soft smile on her lips.

"I did, thank you," Hannah said, shifting in her seat. "I noticed you left my room the same. I felt like a little girl sleeping in there again."

"We didn't have the heart to change it," Grandmother said with a smile, deep wrinkles in her cheeks. "Do you remember when we purchased those hangings for your bed? You refused to sleep there for weeks."

Hannah smiled at the memory. "I crept into your room every night until I grew used to them. Mother was so upset when you wrote to her of my obstinance." Her brow furrowed. "I suppose nothing has changed in that regard."

When Hannah had woken up that morning, she had felt as if she could breathe for the first time in years. There were no plans to entertain callers, no clothes to be decided upon, no shops to visit. She rose without the sound of a servant tapping upon her door at her mother's request. The day lay unfolded before her, to be spent in whatever way she wished, and she relished the thought. She knew Mother would be upset with Hannah's escape to Cornwall, but Hannah could not return to London, not after tasting such freedom and peace again. She *would* not.

Her grandmother's words broke through her thoughts. "We did not have much opportunity to speak last evening. How was your mother before you left? She must be beside herself with worry."

Hannah returned to staring out of the window at the hedges in the distance. "I sent a letter already to let her know I have arrived at the manor safely."

"She will certainly be relieved. Does she still keep you busy, taking you around the whole of London?"

"I'm afraid so."

"Have you spoken to her yet of your dislike for doing so?"

"She knows, but she chooses to ignore my opinion."

Grandmother studied her. "I take it your relationship has not improved then?"

Hannah shrugged. "She has grown more comfortable instructing me in the ways of Society. I have grown more comfortable in merely following along. So I suppose, in a way, our relationship has grown."

She clenched her teeth together to end the bitterness spicing her tongue. Being away from Mother had opened the flood gates to Hannah's true feelings, but she did not wish to upset her grandmother with caustic remarks. She took a deep breath and finished with, "But that is what mothers do, I suppose," and she forced a smile.

Grandmother, however, appeared to see through her feigned joy. "I am sorry, Hannah, that your happiness is not what it should be in London. But do your friends not help? Miss Lewis? And Mr. Hawkins?"

Hannah started, her eyes darting to her grandmother. "Why do you ask after Mr. Hawkins?"

Grandmother pulled back. "Why, I was merely curious. He was over quite often with his mother when we visited last, was he not?"

Of course. Hannah had forgotten. She placed a hand to her chest, her heart racing. "He has been a good friend."

Yes, a friend. But that certainly wasn't what Mother and Mr. Hawkins thought. Hannah wondered if the gentleman had been told that she would consider his proposal. Did that mean an understanding existed between them?

She squirmed in her seat. Mr. Hawkins was a good man. She never should have allowed him such hope.

"Hannah?"

She looked up and noticed her grandmother's watchful gaze upon her. "Yes?"

Grandmother's eyebrows drew together with emotion. "You know your grandfather and I love you, so we cannot help but express to you our concern over your actions. To travel across the country with only your lady's maid to accompany you. Suppose something had happened?"

Hannah focused on the brushes laid out beside her. "I assure you, Grandmama, I had considered all of the repercussions beforehand."

Of course, Hannah had not realized the stupidity of her reckless actions until she had left London. Spending two nights in rather sordid locations had been somewhat unsettling, especially for Daisy. Their specific request for a lock on the door had made each inn owner regard them suspiciously. Her grandmother did not need to know all of that, though.

"The journey was uneventful, at any rate," Hannah continued. "The most disquieting part was when we wandered across the countryside at dark. Until Thomas helped us, of course."

As she chose a small brush with thin bristles, silence resonated in her ears.

"How did you find Thomas after all these years?" Grandmother eventually asked. "He has grown into a fine gentleman, has he not? Rather handsome, I think."

"He was always handsome," Hannah responded. She dipped her brush into a jar of dark green paint.

"And does your mother disapprove of your friendship still?"

"Mother disapproves of everything I do." Hannah flicked her brush along the canvas in short, abrupt swipes. "My eating habits, my posture, my choice in friends, my grandparents—"

She bit her bottom lip, ending her words with a quick glance at her grandmother, but she was already nodding.

"Your grandfather and I are fully aware of your mother's opinion, my dear," she said, "but I assure you, we are no longer going to allow her feelings to keep us from you any longer."

Hannah gave a slight shake of her head. "Keep you from me? What do you mean?"

Grandmother hesitated. "We have asked your mother to allow us to visit you more often, but she has told us that you would prefer to keep our visits to once a year, as you have very little time to spare for us."

Hannah's mouth dropped open. "What? No, no, that isn't true. I was never happier than when the both of you would visit."

"I know, but your mother…" She shook her head. "She brushes aside any mention of you being unhappy in London. We have requested your presence in Cornwall many times, but she has ignored our wishes."

Hannah's mouth parted. "I thought…Mother always said you could hardly afford to visit us, that I would be a burden if I returned to you, just as I was when I was a child."

Grandmother's nostrils flared. She closed her eyes, drawing in a deep breath before speaking again. "You have never been a burden, Hannah, nor will you ever be. Not to us, at any rate. And even if we *were* destitute, that would hardly keep us from you. But as you can see from our freshly-painted entryway to our refurnished parlor, your grandfather and I live very comfortable lives. We can certainly afford a trip to London."

Hannah glanced around her, noting the new mirror and chairs, recalling seeing the newly-painted walls in the entryway, and frowned. How could she have been so naïve? Hannah had been want for nothing growing up, and her grandparents had always been well-off. How could she have ever thought otherwise?

"Your grandfather and I had even considered renting a home in London to be closer to you," Grandmother continued. "We would have asked your opinion about such when you were younger, but we feared your mother would then prevent us from seeing you at all."

Hannah's face burned hot with anger. She knew Mother hated living in Cornwall. She had often told Hannah, "Had my own father done his duty and prevented me from marrying the first man I fell in love with, I would never have married your father, nor moved to such a county." But to have Mother spread lies about Hannah, no doubt in an attempt to sever any final ties the woman had to Cornwall—and her departed husband's family—was despicable.

"How could I have been so stupid?" Hannah asked. "How could I have been so blind as to not see her fabrications?"

"My dear," Grandmother began, "Lady Beatrice always preferred a different life to anything Cornwall and our son could have offered her. But your father was besotted. And we were happy because *he* was happy. Unfortunately, some parents choose to inflict their will on their children, thinking they know better. This can cause a great deal of heartache, though, as you are most keenly aware."

Hannah nodded, unable to speak due to the knot once more in her throat. She focused on swirling her paint brush in a jar of water to clean the paint from its bristles.

"But," her grandmother continued, "I do still believe that your mother loves you. After all, she knew you were happier here in Cornwall when you were a child. That is why she allowed you to remain here for so very long. I believe she has simply lost sight of that in her efforts to rid herself from Cornwall once and for all."

Hannah's shoulders fell forward. "I know you are right. Though, I cannot understand her reasoning, nor can I bear the thought of living under her rule any longer."

"Then you must stay with us. Only if you wish to, of course. You are old enough to make your own decision on the matter now."

A warmth spread throughout Hannah's body. "Are you certain, Grandmama?"

Tears filled Grandmother's blue eyes. "We were blessed to have you in our home from the moment you were born, Hannah. And we missed your bright spirit the moment you left. Nothing would thrill us more than to have you call Rudhek Manor your home again."

They shared teary-eyed smiles, and Hannah breathed a sigh of relief. "Thank you, Grandmama. I was so worried where to turn next. I was considering begging in the streets or becoming your scullery maid. Neither sounded appealing, really."

"No, indeed," her grandmother laughed. "Now, before we move on, I should like to know, what has finally pulled you away from London?"

Hannah's spirits clouded over once again. She chose a brush with smaller bristles and dipped it into a light green shade. "I left because…because Mother asked me to do something I did not have the heart to do."

That was as specific as she cared to be. She hoped her grandmother would understand.

"I see. And did you speak with her about it?"

"I suppose I could have tried a little harder to do so," Hannah said, sliding the paint at the tip of her brush along the dark hedges on her canvas. "But I did not know what I wanted then. In truth, I still don't know now. I just…I needed to get away. I needed to be free. I needed—"

"To see Thomas again."

Hannah opened her mouth, intent on protesting, but her grandmother's twinkling eyes caused an unavoidable smile on her lips.

"I suppose I did," Hannah said, "though Mother will not be pleased to learn I have spent time with him."

"Well your grandfather and I have no qualms with you furthering your relationship with the gentleman. And, now that you are staying here, I don't see any reason why you should *not* see him."

She winked, and Hannah's heart soared. "You are quite right, Grandmama. He has invited me to join him at Tregalwen Beach this evening with a few of his friends and tenants. You and Grandfather are invited to come, of course."

"How very kind of him to offer," Grandmother said.

A frown flickered across Hannah's brow as she wondered if Thomas was merely being polite when he had invited Hannah to the party. But she pushed aside the discouraging thought and removed the lid from the jar of soft blue paint.

"So you will join us then?" she asked.

"I'm sure we would have loved to," her grandmother responded, "but we are already attending a dinner party at Pryvly House. Do you recall Miss Stedman? Her mother has been anxious to find a match for her ever since she was introduced last Season. I'm sure she would be pleased to see you again."

"Perhaps you and I may call on her together another day then?"

For some reason, the thought of paying calls and attending parties in Cornwall did not bother Hannah as greatly as it had in London.

No doubt because she found her grandmother's company more pleasing than her mother's.

"That would be lovely." Grandmother stood from her chair, patting Hannah affectionately upon the cheek. "It is wonderful to have you home, my dear."

Hannah smiled. As Grandmother left the room, she returned to her painting with a happy sigh.

Yes. It was wonderful to finally be home.

CHAPTER FIVE

To stop Hannah from traipsing once more across the countryside, her grandparents had offered to bring her to Tregalwen Beach in their carriage on the way to their dinner party. Hannah had readily agreed, if only to arrive at the beach sooner.

"Would you like us to stop by on our return journey, Hannah, to bring you home?" Grandmother asked as the carriage rolled to a stop.

"Oh, I do not know."

"Of course not, my dear," Grandfather said with a soft pat upon his wife's knee. "Thomas will see her safely home, as he always has."

Hannah smiled. She had very often convinced Thomas to stay out long after dark, purely so she might feign uncertainty across the landscape and have him bring her home on the back of his horse instead. She recalled how it felt to wrap her arms around him from behind, to rest her head upon his back, and she sighed.

"Will you, Hannah?"

She blinked, dazed to see her grandparents' expectant looks in her direction. "Forgive me. Will I what?"

"Will you allow Thomas to see you home?" Grandmother asked.

"Oh, yes, of course."

"There, you see, my dear?" Grandfather said as the carriage door opened, and Hannah scooted forward on her seat.

"You shan't go wandering alone," Grandmother continued, "to be lost in the dark?"

"No, I will not be so impulsive again, I assure you."

Her grandparents exchanged looks.

"Can she make such a promise, do you think?" her grandmother asked.

Grandfather shook his head. "Not if she intends to keep it."

Hannah smiled at their teasing and exited the carriage.

"Do enjoy yourself, Hannah," Grandmother called after her, "and remember, we will wait up for you, as usual."

Hannah poked her head back into the carriage with a smile. "I know."

She backed away, waving goodbye as they set off across the countryside before she turned toward Tregalwen Beach.

Hannah had longed for Cornwall every day for three years, and yet, she did not realize how greatly she had missed her home until she stood, gazing out at the open ocean before her.

The sea shimmered turquoise in the early evening sunlight, and a gentle breeze blew toward her, rippling her soft pink gown. She moved through the tall, wispy grass to where the land sloped slightly down, leading to a wide beach of smooth, cream-colored sand.

She paused, taking in the sights around her before closing her eyes, reminding herself that she was to remain in Cornwall, that the peace she had finally found would not be taken from her again.

The late-August sun warmed her cheeks. She drew in a

deep breath of the salty air. The sound of the endless waves swirled about her. She shifted in the sand, and though her footing seemed unstable, she felt secure. She felt safe.

"Hannah!"

Her heart leapt at the sound of Thomas's voice. She opened her eyes and turned to face him. "Good evening, Thomas."

He walked toward her, and suddenly, she found it difficult to breathe. His broad, handsome smile told her exactly what she wanted to know—Thomas was pleased to see her.

"I see you did not get lost on your way here," he said.

Hannah smiled. "No, my grandparents offered me a ride in their carriage."

"Ah," Thomas said, and he stopped before her.

Their eyes met, and Hannah wondered what he thought as he studied her face. He blinked, seeming to come out of a daze before motioning toward the north end of the beach. "Shall we join the others? I'm sure you will remember most of them."

She nodded, and they walked together toward the small group gathered around a large fire crackling upon the sand. Thomas led her first to a gentleman with a graying beard and warm, blue eyes.

"You remember Mr. Moore," Thomas said, "the keeper of Golowduyn Lighthouse."

"Of course," Hannah said. The gentleman had once led her and her grandparents around in a small tour of Golowduyn many years prior. He had explained to them how he had left the world behind to live in Cornwall, and Hannah recalled admiring his decision. "How fares your lighthouse, sir?"

"She shines every night and through every storm," Mr. Moore said brightly, "so we are happy."

A woman a few years older than Hannah moved to stand next to Mr. Moore, her auburn hair in a loose, lopsided bun.

Hannah recognized her at once as Mr. Moore's niece,

Abigail, whose reserved nature and clear discomfort with being near others had obviously remained the same over the years.

"Uncle, Mr. Sheffield needs your help moving the spit," Abigail said in a hushed tone.

Mr. Moore excused himself from Hannah and Thomas, and as he left, Abigail followed him, speaking to Hannah as she backed away. "Miss Summerfield, you have returned to Cornwall at last."

"I have," Hannah said with a glance in Thomas's direction, his eyes catching hers as he smiled. "I trust you are well, Miss Moore."

"Yes, thank you." She averted her gaze, still walking away as she spoke over her shoulder. "If you will excuse me, I must help my uncle."

She shifted her feet in the sand in a slight curtsy and scurried away.

"Uncle Ellis," Hannah overheard the woman say as she tugged at Mr. Moore's sleeve, "may I return to Golowduyn now?"

"We have only just arrived, Abigail," Mr. Moore responded. "Please, stay a little while longer."

Their conversation faded from Hannah's ears as Thomas brought her to the others, until one by one, she was introduced and welcomed by all in attendance.

The relaxed atmosphere contrasted drastically to the charged energy Hannah had experienced in Town for so long, but she knew in an instant which life she preferred. The dancing, loud music, and overly polite society in London had drained her spirits. She had longed for honest company, real conversation, and easy smiles, what she had always experienced with Thomas.

As they conversed on Tregalwen with his tenants, neighbors, and friends, Hannah could not help but stare at his handsome smile.

Yes, she far preferred a life in Cornwall with Thomas.

As the sinking sun colored the beach a golden orange, the roasted duck and pheasant were divvied up on plates with boiled potatoes and carrots and then distributed amongst the guests.

Hannah and Thomas sat down beside each other on one of the thick logs that had been dragged from the top of the beach to circle around the fire.

"Are you enjoying yourself so far?" Thomas asked as he balanced his plate in one hand and ate with the other.

"Oh, very much," Hannah replied with an eager nod. "It seems a lifetime ago since we enjoyed one of these parties together."

"And now I am the host instead of my father."

Hannah's smile faded away. Thomas had written Hannah with news of his father's death months after her departure to London, and her heart had ached for him. His mother had died mere days after Thomas's birth, and without siblings, he had no family to comfort him. Hannah had asked for permission to return to Cornwall then, but Mother had insisted that Thomas needed time to grieve. How Hannah regretted not standing up to her. She should have been there at Thomas's side, to let him know he was not alone.

"I was so sorry to hear from you that he passed," she said softly. "I wanted to come to his funeral, but…"

Thomas merely nodded as her words faded away. She studied him for a moment before looking at the group of people gathered around them.

"I am sure he would be very pleased with you continuing this tradition," she said, motioning to the others. "Friends joining together for wonderful food and pleasant company. A chance to rest from their cares and troubles. He was always proud of you, and I'm certain he would be still."

"I hope so." Thomas looked at her with his warm gaze. "Thank you, Hannah."

She cleared her throat. "Although, I think he would be rather displeased that you are socializing with me once again. Your father was not partial to me, I'm afraid."

"That isn't true." Thomas stared at his plate. "But your mother is not partial to *me*." Hannah looked up at his sorrowful eyes. "That is why we stopped writing, was it not? Because your mother did not approve of you corresponding with a gentleman who could never be as fine as those in London?"

Hannah struggled to find the right words, but what could she say when the truth was so obvious? The relaxed feeling between them faded away, reality settling in around her, and her shoulders fell.

She stared down at her plate of food, moving to pick at a potato before realizing she wore her gloves. Mother had never allowed her out in public without them, so Hannah had habitually put them on that evening.

With a lip curled in disgust, she pulled her fingers free of the white silk, draping the gloves across her lap with a shake of her head.

"Mother and I agree on very little," she said. Her words were soft, and she wondered if Thomas had heard them before he responded.

"And yet, you must have agreed in some regard. No doubt you both were in approval when you stopped writing me."

Hannah stared at him blankly. "Why, no. My mother encouraged me, of course, but I only stopped writing because *you* did."

He glanced at her sidelong. "Forgive me, Hannah, but I find that difficult to believe. I distinctly remember the last letter I sent to you, and the lack of response I received from it."

She narrowed her eyes. "No, I remember your last letter, as well. You wrote to me of the success you had in growing your crops that year."

"No, I wrote to ask you if I could…" His words ended in a sigh, and he shook his head.

Hannah's heart thudded against her chest. "To ask if you could what?" When Thomas hesitated again, she pushed further. "What did you ask, Thomas?"

Finally, he met her gaze, an uncharacteristic vulnerability in his eyes. "I asked if I could come visit you in London."

"You what?" Hannah breathed.

Thomas continued. "You did not reply, so I gathered you did not wish me to come. I assumed ignoring my letter was the easiest way for you to inform me of such."

Instantly, Hannah shook her head. Thomas had wanted to come to London to see her? She could hardly believe it. "I assure you, Thomas, I never received such a letter."

"You didn't?"

She could hear the hesitance in his tone and see it in his eyes. "No," she said firmly. "Never."

But why had she not? A strange tension crept up her spine, and she nearly groaned. "Mother." Of course it was her doing. Hannah should have known.

"What about your mother?" Thomas asked.

Hannah shook her head with dismay. "She must have taken your letters before I had the chance to see them. When I received no further word from you, I thought you wished to end our friendship. That is when I stopped writing, as well."

"How could you ever think that was true?" he asked.

Hannah winced. "The same way you could think I did not wish you to visit me in London."

Their eyes met. Years of pain, of misunderstanding and heartache, hung between them. Neither of them had meant for their correspondence to end, neither of them had wished to hurt the other, but the damage had been done. Hannah could not help but long for the past when she and Thomas had spoken openly, comfortably. Before her intrusive mother had stretched her icy fingers around Hannah, altering her life and Thomas's.

She glanced to Thomas, his eyes still upon her.

"I suppose we would be better off not dwelling on the past," he said. "Unless, of course, we think instead on the trouble we caused as children." He paused, a soft smile curving his lips. "Do you remember how we used to explore the coves for buried treasure?"

Hannah nodded, grateful for the change in topics. "Of course."

Thomas's smile grew. "Baldwin could not comprehend where all of the silverware had gone."

Hannah shook her head, imagining the bewildered look upon the face of the Causeys' butler. "Yet another one of your servants who must simply despise me. And for good reason."

"Well what else were we to use to dig the holes?" Thomas asked. "We needed the smaller spoons to not damage the gold we were going to come across."

"We could have at least brought them back to him. I'm sure if we go exploring in those old coves again, we'd find a whole set." She beamed at his deep laughter, the tension from before fading away. "We did get into a fair bit of mischief, didn't we? And it only grew as we did. Do you remember how we used to hide when my grandparents and your father would come out looking for us? The fields near your house proved very useful."

"As did the hedges near the manor."

"And that last summer, when they learned where to find us," Hannah continued, "we took to sneaking out when everyone else had fallen asleep—"

"And met here, at Tregalwen."

A sigh escaped her lips. "How I loved those nights, huddled together near the small fires you built, attempting to scare each other with tales of ghosts and other creatures of the night."

"Always at your suggestion," Thomas added.

"That *was* my idea, wasn't it?" Hannah had not particularly enjoyed the ghost stories, but she *did* love the excuse to hold onto his arm as they frightened one another in the dark.

She struggled to fight off the sadness threatening to come over her again as she thought of how simple her childhood had been. Would they ever escape the weight placed upon them both by her mother's actions?

"The mischievous ideas usually were yours," Thomas said. "But I followed along without hesitation."

Hannah paused, narrowing her eyes at him and tilting her head to one side. "Why *did* you always follow along, Thomas?"

The look in his eyes caused a fluttering in her stomach. "You know very well, Hannah, I never had the heart to tell you no."

His eyes, a golden green in the gilded sun, flickered to her lips, and her pulse quickened.

"There is one thing, though, that I always suggested," he said, putting down his plate, "that *you* could never say no to." He smiled in her direction, a daring flash in his eyes. "What do you say to a horse race across the beach?"

CHAPTER SIX

Thomas watched as Hannah's eyes lit with excitement.

"A horse race? Now?" she questioned.

He nodded. "If I remember correctly, you mentioned, when last we met upon these shores, that you wished to race me on horseback. And I believe you said you intended to win."

She covered her face with her hands. "Oh, don't remind me. I would never have made such a bold declaration had I known what my life would be like in London. I had very little time to ride at all."

"Your excuses shall not save you, Hannah," he said, relishing the sight of her dimples deepening with her smile.

"Excuses? They are facts, Thomas!" she said with a laugh. "I don't have a horse, my gown is hardly suitable for riding, and I really have not ridden in months. Indeed, I was supposed to go with Mr. Hawkins and his friends, but I left before I could."

A strange knot settled in his stomach. "Mr. Hawkins?"

Hannah's face drained of all color, her eyes wide with

shock. "Er, yes," she stammered, "the, the son of my mother's friend."

"Oh," was all he said.

He could see her scrambling to change the subject, and a wariness washed over him. She had never mentioned any Mr. Hawkins in her early letters. Whoever he was, she had clearly not meant to mention him, and she obviously did not want to speak of him further.

Her grandparents had said that Hannah was not attached to another, but what if she had fallen in love only recently? Her mother, after all, must have pushed for an arrangement in London. The woman seemed to stop at nothing to prevent her daughter from placing permanent roots in Cornwall.

Ignoring the heavy weight settling on his chest, Thomas fought again to capture the lighthearted feeling between them. "So, Hannah, do you accept my challenge of a race then?"

She smiled weakly. "I don't think I can, Thomas."

His happiness threatened to dash away at her refusal, but he shook his head, clicking his tongue with disappointment. "I never thought I would see the day when Hannah Summerfield would refuse a challenge. I was wrong earlier. Being in London *has* changed you."

A pained expression flashed across her face, and he watched her bury the tips of her boots into the sand.

Thomas's smile faded away. Had his teasing truly offended her? Or was she simply lingering on the gentleman she mentioned before or her mother's despicable actions?

"I'm sorry," he said, pushing aside thoughts of the woman before his anger grew at her meddling. "I did not mean to upset you, Hannah."

She shook her head. "No, you are right. I have become someone I hardly recognize. But I think I should like to try to return to who I was before. Excepting, of course, being a thief of silverware."

Thomas grinned as she set her half-eaten plate of food

next to her and leapt to her feet. Her gloves that had been resting across her lap fell to the sand. The twinkle in her eye resembled how she appeared in the doorway of Leighton House, carefree, filled with joy, and his heart skipped a beat.

"Mr. Causey, I accept your challenge." She paused. "Oh, but I may need to borrow a horse. And a sidesaddle."

She looked around her as Thomas stood. "I brought two geldings with me to carry the food from Leighton House," he said. "You may ride one of them, if you like. And as for a sidesaddle..." He looked to where a saddled blue roan was tied near his own horses. "That one will do nicely."

Together, they walked to the other side of the fire, approaching Abigail, who sat forward with her chin on her palm, her other hand playing with a stray lock of her auburn hair.

"Miss Moore?" Thomas began. The woman glanced up at them with indifference. "Might you allow Miss Summerfield the use of your sidesaddle for a moment?"

Abigail pulled a face. "Whatever for?"

"Mr. Causey here has challenged me to a race across the beach," Hannah explained, drawing the attention of those around them. "You see, he won every race we had as children, and I should like the opportunity now to humble him."

"I need to leave for the lighthouse," Abigail said, her gaze averted before she glanced up at Hannah with a half-smile, "but I suppose it can wait another moment or two."

While the sidesaddle was moved from Abigail's horse to one of Thomas's, news of the race traveled throughout the gathering. Mr. Moore pulled a stick across the sand to create a starting point. Several children began a footrace of their own across the beach. A few others gathered around where the race would begin while the older couples in attendance stood by with amused expressions.

Thomas watched Hannah toss her bonnet and shawl atop her gloves in the sand.

"You *are* determined this evening," he said.

With a raised brow, he removed his jacket and rolled up the sleeves of his shirt. Hannah laughed joyfully in response.

They mounted the dark brown horses behind the line in the sand, and Mr. Moore counted down from three. Thomas glanced at Hannah. They shared a smile before the signal was given, and they set off in a swirl of sand.

His larger horse easily pulled ahead, and Thomas couldn't help but laugh as he leaned forward over the saddle, the wind against his body, rippling his shirt.

After a moment, he looked over his shoulder, intent on reveling in his quick success with a teasing smile, just as he always had. However, when he caught sight of Hannah riding toward him, her hair falling from its chignon one lost pin at a time, her cheeks rosy, and eyes as bright as her smile, his pulse raced.

He had often seen that very look of delight, of freedom, in her expression when they were children. He had been helpless when Hannah had smiled in such a way, and he was still helpless now, for even his grown heart melted at the sight.

As he thought of the love he still had for her, he discreetly tugged on the reins.

CHAPTER SEVEN

Hannah overtook Thomas mere moments before they passed the monolith.

"Well done, Hannah! Well done."

She slowed her horse, looking over her shoulder to see Thomas's congratulatory smile as he trotted toward her. Only then did she notice his horse standing a few hands taller than her own.

"There is nothing quite like riding across the beach, is there?" she asked between heavy breaths, setting her suspicions aside as she patted her horse's dark brown neck. The horse nickered in response, and Hannah smiled. How wonderful it felt to ride again, to feel the powerful animal carrying her across the sand.

Cheers from behind her sounded, and she looked to see a few of the children running toward them with wide smiles.

"Such fine riding!" one boy called out.

"Did ye truly win, miss?" asked another.

"Yes, yes," Thomas said, "Miss Summerfield has finally beaten me. Let us move on. I should like to forget this ever happened."

He winked at Hannah, and she narrowed her eyes. His

nonchalant manner revealed the truth about their race, but she decided to keep her newfound knowledge to herself.

When they returned to the others, Hannah received their compliments graciously, eying Thomas's unfailing smile as they teased him for his loss. Soon, however, the excitement died down, and the group gathered once more around the fire.

The sun had just begun its descent into the silver-blue sea, causing a chill to come upon the air. Hannah retrieved her shawl, pulling the cover around her shoulders. Her bonnet and gloves lay forgotten on the sand as she moved to sit next to Thomas on the same log situated near the outer edge of the group.

"So," Thomas said as he nudged her shoulder with his own, "how do you feel after winning at last?"

As his lips curved with his secretive smile, Hannah shook her head. "I know you let me win, Thomas Causey."

He feigned ignorance. "What do you mean?"

Folding her arms across her chest, she gave him an incredulous look. "Your horse is clearly larger than the one I rode, and as I mentioned earlier, I haven't ridden for months. There is no earthly way I could have won."

"Yes, there is. You are simply a natural."

"No, you were always a better rider than I was." She sighed. "At any rate, I am grateful you allowed me one brief, thrilling moment where I was able to feel as you have always felt. It was rather…freeing."

She had not experienced the sensation in years. As she stared out at the sea, a soberness came upon her, and she feared her peace, her freedom, was only temporary. Yes, she was to remain in Cornwall with her grandparents, but she would one day have to face Mother and Mr. Hawkins, and at the thought, she struggled to maintain the feeling of joy she had felt before.

"Hannah, may I ask you a question?"

At Thomas's serious tone, Hannah's fingers clenched her shawl, her stomach tying in knots. "Of course."

"I understand that your mother wished you to remain in London," he began carefully. "However, as you did not particularly enjoy your time there and so obviously longed for Cornwall, why did you wait until now to return? It does not seem like you to not fight for something you desire."

She dropped her gaze. "You said it yourself, Thomas. London has changed me. My *mother* has changed me. I wanted to leave, but she convinced me that I was not wanted in Cornwall any longer. And now, I have tried to be who I was before, but I cannot. There is too much holding me back."

Thomas shook his head, leaning toward her. "You said before that my father disliked you, but in truth, he always admired your tenacity. Before he died, he told me that he feared your mother would change you. He said the whole of Cornwall seemed to know of Lady Beatrice's dislike for the county when she had lived here. He hated to think you would be urged into feeling the same way." Thomas reached for Hannah's hand and grasped it in his own. "But I told him he was wrong, that you would never stop loving Cornwall. Hannah, you may have lost yourself for a time, but you need only allow Cornwall, and those who care for you, to help you return. *Truly* return."

Hannah stared at his hand holding hers, his touch sending pleasant tingles up and down her skin. He was right, of course. If she simply spoke with him, told him the truth about her mother and Mr. Hawkins, she was certain he could help her find the courage to face them both. After all, he had always helped her before. Why would it be any different now?

"Thomas," she began, "I would like to speak with you about something."

He leaned forward, his eyes intently focused.

"I mentioned Mr. Hawkins before." She swallowed. "Well, he and I...That is, my mother—"

Her words were interrupted by rhythmic clapping across the fire, and they looked to see Mr. Moore leading the group in a song.

Thomas faced her again with a disappointed look, but she smiled.

"We can speak afterward," she said with an encouraging nod.

In truth, she was relieved to postpone the discussion. She would much rather enjoy her evening with Thomas without another thought of London, or who still expected her return.

Pushing aside her gloomy musings, Hannah switched her attention to the singing. She longed to join in with the others, but time had worn her memory, so she simply hummed, clapped, and swayed along.

When she noticed Thomas not singing either, she leaned closer to him. "Do you not sing anymore?"

"I do," he responded, "but I am merely...distracted this evening."

Hannah eyed him curiously, wondering at his sunken shoulders.

The song ended, and another round of cheering ensued.

"Choose the next for us, Causey!" Mr. Moore called out from across the fire.

Thomas glanced sidelong at Hannah. "*Tykki Duw*, sir."

"*Tykki Duw*!" Mr. Moore repeated.

Hannah smiled. She had always enjoyed the song. Had Thomas remembered?

She shifted her weight on the log to make herself more comfortable, unintentionally bringing herself closer to him, her shoulder grazing his.

The song began. Thomas's voice joined in with the others, and Hannah listened to the lyrics as if for the first time.

She flew by in a flutter, a breath on the breeze,
Her black and orange wings flying high 'midst the trees.

I beckoned her t'ward me with an outstretched hand,
And upon my finger did she gracefully land.

I brought her with me, to flowers so sweet.
I had her trust. I would ne'er mistreat.
But a strong wind blew and pulled her away,
So I watched and waited as the sky grew gray.

Grow strong, tykki duw, fly far, tykki duw.
Leave me here, as we know you must do.
Go with the wind, to a new land,
Where'er it may be, howe'er so grand.
But please, don't forget home, nor those who love you,
And return to me, my beloved tykki duw.

Hannah had always loved hearing Thomas sing, but as she listened to his deep voice, a stirring occurred in her soul. In London, she had often thought she might have imagined her feelings for her lifelong friend. However, since her return to Cornwall, every moment she had spent in his company had only reinforced the love she had always had for him. There was no one who made her feel such joy, no one who listened to her as he did, who encouraged her own happiness, and loved her just as she was.

She knew, as she finally accepted that love, she could not be parted from him again.

I looked each day for her return,
Waiting and hoping, long did I yearn.
In my garden of milkweed and roses so pink,
The longer I waited, the further I'd sink.

Until, at last, I saw her fly o'er t'ward me,
Past the old mines and near the blue sea.
She landed on my finger, just like before.

And I stared at her colors as we stood on the moor.

Her wings were limp, though her colors still shone
As bright as any sunset I had ever known.
But still, she was weak, could hardly stand,
So I carried her home in the palm of my hand.

She felt Thomas's knee press softly against her leg. Her skin numbed from the warmth of his touch. Slowly, she allowed her eyes to travel the length of him, and her breath caught in her throat as his hazel eyes watched her while he sang.

You were strong, tykki duw.
You've flown far, tykki duw.
You've left me here, as you knew you needed to.
You went with the wind to a faraway land,
But I know where you went was not so grand.
For you did not forget home, nor I, who love you,
And you returned to me, my beloved, my beloved tykki duw.

Those gathered around the fire repeated the last verse, but Thomas had stopped singing, his eyes focused on her lips.

Slowly, the other voices faded away, the crackling fire and the sea's waves the only sounds reaching her ears. Thomas placed a finger beneath her chin, gently tilting her head back as he leaned toward her.

Her eyes fluttered closed, and her heart stilled. She felt his nose brush against her cheek first, then his breath was upon her lips, and she waited eagerly, impatiently, as he hovered just out of reach.

Just then, the song ended and more cheers erupted, breaking apart the euphoria his nearness had created. Hannah jerked away, ducking her head at once. Heat flushed through her body, and she darted her eyes to those around the fire.

Thankfully, no one seemed aware of what had nearly occurred between her and Thomas, except a few young girls who sat nearby, giggling behind their hands with wide eyes.

She looked sidelong at Thomas. He raked his fingers through his hair, the muscles in his jaw twitching.

Another song began, and he leaned close, his breath upon her ear. "Next time, I will not choose so public a place. I promise you that." He caught her gaze with a wink before joining in the next song.

Hannah unconsciously wet her lips and loosened her shawl from around her shoulders, the fire feeling suddenly warm.

A range of emotions washed over her. Disappointment that the kiss had not occurred. Guilt for Mr. Hawkins hoping a marriage might be possible with her. Frustration with her mother for meddling so fiercely in her life. And mostly anger toward herself for not returning to Cornwall sooner, thereby avoiding all that upset her.

As the night wore on, she attempted to set aside her emotions, focusing instead on Thomas singing with the others. The party continued until the last log turned to ash, stifled yawns interrupted the singing, and everyone began to disperse.

Thomas's servants were tasked to return to Leighton House with the cooking supplies on the spare horse, so Hannah had no choice but to ride double with Thomas.

Not that she had any complaint. In fact, as she sat in front of him, his arms wrapped securely around her, she did not think she had ever felt so content.

The moon shone across the countryside, the only sounds being that of the horse's steady gait beneath them and the ocean's waves behind them.

As they continued, she rested her head upon his shoulder and pressed her nose against his neck.

"Hannah?"

She felt his deep voice vibrate softly in his throat, and she lazily hummed a response.

"What were you saying before, about your mother…and Mr. Hawkins?" he asked.

Hannah winced. She did not wish to speak about such matters. She wanted time to simply enjoy the closeness with the man she loved, untainted with worrying thoughts. There would be time to speak yet.

She kept her mouth closed, pretending she was already fast asleep.

"Hannah?"

She bit her lip, forcing her breathing to remain steady until he rested his cheek upon the top of her head, and her heart swelled with love.

Only a moment seemed to pass by before the lights from Rudhek Manor glowed behind her closed eyes.

"We're here, Hannah," Thomas softly said, and she raised her head from his shoulder.

"Already?"

"I'm afraid so."

The husky tone to his voice caused her heart to flutter, but she dared not look up at him.

He helped her slide down from the horse before he dismounted, and together they walked toward the front door, stopping to face each other at the bottom of the manor's stairs.

Butterflies took flight in her stomach as Thomas reached for her hand, stroking his thumb back and forth across her skin.

"Hannah," he began, pausing a moment after.

"Yes?" she breathed. Was he going to repeat his question? Or would he attempt to kiss her again?

"These last few years," he continued, "the months we have spent apart, I don't know how I…"

He paused, turning his head to where the hedges lined the drive, and his brow furrowed.

"What is it?" she asked, facing the same direction.

The pounding of horse hooves reached her ears, the gait slowing as the horse clopped across the gravel, and she narrowed her eyes to see into the darkness.

"Who could be coming here at so late an hour?" she muttered.

Thomas didn't respond.

The rider neared, but his face was shadowed beneath his tall hat. He pulled his snorting horse to a stop nearby, and Hannah took in the sight of the chestnut stallion, the white snippet at the end of its nose glowing from the light of the manor. She drew in a sharp breath, removing her hand from Thomas's and taking a step back.

The horse was impossible to mistake, and when the gentleman dismounted and removed his hat, Hannah's heart lurched.

"Mr. Hawkins."

CHAPTER EIGHT

Thomas's eyes snapped to Hannah's. Mr. Hawkins? This was the man she had spoken of earlier? His mouth grew dry.

"Good evening, Miss Summerfield," the tall gentleman said in a rigid tone.

"Mr. Hawkins," she repeated, taking another subtle step away from Thomas, "what are you doing here?"

Exactly what Thomas was thinking. What was the gentleman doing there, so late at night, interrupting his time with Hannah?

"I apologize for my unannounced arrival, Miss Summerfield," the gentleman said, his eyes skirting from Thomas to Hannah. "I was tasked by your mother to ensure you arrived at your grandparents safely."

Thomas cocked his head. Really? The gentleman traveled for days and through the dark to see if Hannah was safe…all for her mother? His insides churned.

"Well, as you can see, I have," Hannah responded, her eyes focused on the gravel beneath them.

Thomas studied her arms crossed over her body as she chewed on her lower lip. He turned to the gentleman and noted his rigid posture. "Mr. Thomas Causey, sir. Miss Summerfield's childhood friend." Friend. He cringed at the word. "You, I take it, are Mr. Hawkins?"

"Yes." Mr. Hawkins eyed him with a lowered brow. "A pleasure."

They exchanged stiff bows before the door to the manor opened, and light flooded around them. Their eyes fell upon Hannah's grandmother, whose figure was silhouetted as she stood in the doorway.

"I thought I heard voices." She paused. "Mr. Hawkins, is that you? My goodness, what a surprise." She reached a hand to her throat and looked to her granddaughter. "Hannah, you did not tell me you were expecting any visitors from London."

"I did not know he was coming, Grandmama."

Thomas shook his head at her soft voice. Where was his Hannah? Vibrant, confident, full-of-life, Hannah? Anger filled him as he thought of how restrictive her mother must have been to make Hannah so timid and compliant. But what else had happened in London to have altered her so greatly?

He looked back to Mr. Hawkins, whose eyes flickered between Thomas and Hannah again, and Thomas's shoulders stooped forward.

Of course. Hannah was uncomfortable with Mr. Hawkins's arrival because she had not yet had the chance to tell Thomas that she had formed a relationship with the gentleman. That must have been what she was about to say before the music had started up earlier that night.

A terrible ache mangled his heart. First his letters had been stolen by her mother, and now Hannah had been taken by the gentleman standing before him.

Mrs. Summerfield's voice broke through the silence. "Well, there is no need to stand out here in the chilly night air. Why don't you all come in for a cup of tea?"

"Yes, Grandmother," Hannah said, turning at once to go indoors.

Thomas cringed at her instant obedience. "Thank you for the offer, but I must be on my way. Hannah?" Her feet stopped, her head hanging down. "Thank you for joining me this evening."

She did not meet his gaze. "Good night, Mr. Causey." And she continued inside.

Thomas's heart sank in his chest. He looked to Mr. Hawkins. The gentleman eyed him with a narrowed gaze before following Hannah inside.

Thomas mounted his horse and clicked his tongue. His horse's hooves crunched in the gravel one slow step at a time until he heard Mrs. Summerfield calling after him, and he urged his horse to stop.

"Thomas, will you wait just a moment?"

He glanced over his shoulder to see Mrs. Summerfield hastening her step toward him through the darkness. "Did you need something, Mrs. Summerfield?"

"No, I simply wished to thank you for bringing Hannah home," she said. "I trust you had an enjoyable evening."

Thomas thought back to their horse race, the kiss they had nearly shared, and the ride back home with Hannah's soft breath against his neck as she had pretended to sleep to avoid their conversation. The conversation in which she might have told him of her feelings for Mr. Hawkins.

He could only nod in response.

"Good," Mrs. Summerfield said with a strained smile.

Switching the reins to his other hand, Thomas averted his gaze. "Mrs. Summerfield, forgive my prying, but is there something between Mr. Hawkins and Hannah? An understanding, perhaps?"

"Oh, Thomas, I am so sorry," she said, her voice filling with compassion, "but I really couldn't say. That is, I do not know. They were friends in London, but Hannah hardly seemed pleased with his arrival tonight." She rubbed the base of her throat. "In an effort to be transparent, though

Hannah's mother has mentioned before what a fine pair Hannah and Mr. Hawkins would make, were they to ever marry."

Thomas groaned inwardly. Of course her mother would support their union. Mr. Hawkins was unquestionably rich, of fine breeding, no doubt inheriting an estate *not* in Cornwall, and, best of all, he was not Thomas.

How could he have been so stupid as to think Hannah would not have made an attachment in three years? That was no doubt why she looked so fearful whenever London was mentioned. Indeed, that was perhaps the very reason she had pulled away from his kiss. He was a total and absolute fool.

"Thank you, Mrs. Summerfield," he muttered. "If you will excuse me."

He turned away from the woman's wrinkled brow and urged his horse into a trot. His lips stretched in a grim line, and he rode away without a glance back.

CHAPTER NINE

Sleep had evaded Hannah for most of the night. In the early morning, she sat on the window seat in her room, a heavy blanket over her crossed legs. Her head rested against the cool window as she stared at the clouds blanketing the sky in thick, gray sheets.

When she was a child, she would sit in a similar way every morning, watching expectantly for Thomas to appear beyond the ridge on his horse. He would wave to her the moment he spotted her, and she would race immediately to join him before anyone else in the manor had risen.

But that morning was different, for Hannah knew Thomas would not come to her. In truth, she wondered if he would wish to speak with her at all after how the previous night had ended.

Unable to stand her own misery any longer, Hannah jumped down from the window seat, ignoring the untouched tray of food Daisy had brought up to her earlier, and dressed herself in the gown she had worn the day before.

Her step was quick as she marched downstairs. She was anxious to leave before a certain gentleman—who had stayed in one of the manor's spare rooms the night before—had the chance to see her.

"Are you leaving, Hannah?"

Hannah started, whirling around in the entryway to see her grandfather sitting on a chair pressed up against the wall near the staircase. She paused, her hand frozen on the latch of the front door.

"Oh, I did not see you there," she said, releasing her hold of the handle. Her heart thumped dully in her ears. "Yes, I was merely going to stretch my legs for a moment."

"Will you not be cold without a wrap?"

Hannah glanced down at her thin dress, having forgotten her shawl.

"I don't mind the cold," she murmured. "Why are you sitting there?"

A smile played about his lips. "I know you well, my dear. I simply wished to speak with you before you left the manor early, as you used to."

Her cheeks burned.

"Are you going to meet Thomas?"

"I thought I might seek him out," she said.

"Good. I think you ought to."

Her brow raised in surprise. "You do?"

"Yes, but perhaps you might see to a few things before doing so."

She sighed, her shoulders slumped forward. "Must I?"

He chuckled, the warm sound lifting her spirits. He patted the seat next to him, and she crossed the distance to sit beside him. "Have I ever told you that you are my favorite grandchild?" he asked.

"I am your *only* grandchild."

"That is beside the point." His eyes twinkled. "Now, my dear Hannah, your grandmother told me what occurred last evening. Mr. Hawkins's arrival, you leaving him in the entryway the moment you entered the house. Tell me, why did you respond in such a way?"

Hannah traced the lines of the flooring with her eyes. "I was merely surprised to see him here, that is all." She could see his disbelieving look from the corner of her eye.

"Is he, perhaps, the reason you left London?"

"In part, yes." She lowered her voice. "You see, Mother told me that Mr. Hawkins loves me and wishes to seek my hand in marriage. So I left."

"Without a second thought."

She rested her elbow on the armrest, her chin atop her fisted hand. "As you said, you know me well, Grandpapa. I know I should have spoken with them about how I felt concerning the matter, but I panicked. I felt I had no other choice but to agree with what my mother asked of me, so I told her I would consider marrying him. I'm certain she has told Mr. Hawkins of what I said, as well."

"I take it then you do not wish to marry him?"

"Mother thinks I ought to."

"But do you love him?"

She opened her mouth. Every vein in her body screamed the answer, but she merely shrugged. "I ought to, according to Mother."

Her grandfather appeared thoughtful before reaching out to take her hand in his. "Each time your grandmother and I visited you in Town, we would discuss how much you had changed. Of course, you have grown into a beautiful young woman, one we are proud to call our granddaughter. However, it appeared to us that a certain spark in your eye had diminished, and the skip in your step, vanished. It upset us. Greatly."

Tears sprung to Hannah's eyes, and she looked to the ceiling, blinking fiercely to keep her emotions at bay.

"The moment you arrived in Cornwall, though," he continued, "we saw a glimpse of your blue eyes shining like they used to. We finally felt as if our little Hannah had come home to us."

She looked at him and saw the moisture brimming in his own eyes, the color the same shade of blue as hers.

"And I cannot help but wonder," Grandfather said, "if the light returning to your eyes is due to you being in Cornwall or because you have finally been reunited with Thomas."

Tears spilled down Hannah's cheeks, her voice breaking as she spoke. "Both. It has always been both." Her chin quivered. "Oh, Grandpapa, I don't know what to do. I'm certain Thomas thinks there is something between Mr. Hawkins and I, and Mr. Hawkins might believe the very same. But I cannot marry him, no matter how greatly Mother pressures me to do so." Her stomach churned. "Oh, but how is she to stand the gossip that will arise when we do not marry? All of London will surely know. And what if your names are tarnished here, as well, for having such a fickle granddaughter? But then, if I do accept—"

"My dear," her grandfather interrupted softly, "to put others before yourself is a noble cause, but when the deed prevents one's own happiness, nothing but misery follows for everyone involved." He withdrew a handkerchief from his jacket and wiped away her tears. "Tell me now. What is it *you* want?"

Hannah paused. What did *she* want? What *did* she want? For so long, she had done what Mother had expected, and she had lost herself in the process. She had not truly considered her own desires in three years.

Images of her mother's disapproving frown and Mr. Hawkins's hurt expression bounced around in her mind until she finally managed to clear her thoughts. And when she did, all that was left behind were Thomas's hazel eyes and ready smile.

Her chest swelled. She raised her chin and nodded. She knew exactly what she wanted.

"I want to be with Thomas."

Grandfather smiled, his wrinkles deepening. "There you are." He patted her hand. "Now, you know what must be done."

She nodded, wiping away her remaining tears, courage replacing any lingering fears. "Yes, I must speak with him, tell him the truth."

A breathlessness rose up within her, her chest filling with hope. Finally, she felt like the person she was before she had left, only more confident and determined in her desire to be with Thomas.

"I will go to him now." She stood, but her grandfather softly grasped her wrist to prevent her from leaving.

"There is someone else who also deserves the truth, Hannah," he whispered as he stood, "even before Thomas."

His eyes motioned behind her, and she glanced back to see Mr. Hawkins emerge at the top of the stairs, dark circles beneath his eyes.

Her heart dropped, and she turned back to her grandfather. "Now?"

He nodded. "Now, flower."

With an encouraging smile, he disappeared down the side corridor, and Hannah turned around to face Mr. Hawkins, willing herself to remember who she was…and who she loved.

CHAPTER TEN

Mr. Hawkins bowed when he reached the bottom of the stairs. "Miss Summerfield."

"Good morning, Mr. Hawkins," she said. "I trust you slept well."

"I did, thank you," he responded with strained politeness. "Your grandparents were generous enough to offer me a room."

Hannah nodded, noting the dismal curve of his lips, the lines creasing his brow. Her stomach churned. Mr. Hawkins's friendship had been a welcome distraction to the misery she had felt in London, and for that, she would be forever grateful. She did not wish to hurt him, but her grandfather was right. The man deserved the truth.

She faced him squarely. "Mr. Hawkins, I must apologize for last night. You rode a great distance to seek after my well-being, and I did not express to you my gratitude for you doing so. I am sorry."

Mr. Hawkins shook his head. "All is well. I could see you were preoccupied."

"I was. And I admit, I am still. And I now beg your forgiveness for what I am about to say, as it—"

"Please," Mr. Hawkins interrupted, "you must allow me to speak first. I have come here to make my intentions known concerning the future of our relationship."

"Mr. Hawkins, don't," she gently pleaded.

"But I must, Miss Summerfield," he continued, his dark blue eyes focusing on the chandelier, the flooring, the banister, anywhere but her. "This is why I have come all the way from London, to ask for your hand in marriage."

Hannah winced. Why did he have to say it? Could he not see how she wished him to remain silent? She perused his face, wondering how to refuse the man gently, before she noticed the color of his cheeks turning slightly gray.

"Mr. Hawkins, are…are you ill?"

"I am well. I merely await your reply."

Confusion swirled within her. Why did he appear so woeful? Was he not happy to propose? Perhaps he knew she meant to reject him, but how?

"Forgive me," she began delicately. "I am quite flattered at your proposal, but I fear I must refuse you."

He took a step back with a puzzled brow. "Refuse me? May I ask why?"

Her tone was firm, but she spoke the words carefully. "Because I love another."

Mr. Hawkins blanched, his eyes rounding. "Your friend, Mr. Causey?"

She blushed. "Yes."

"Ah," he managed to mutter. "May I ask how long you have loved him?"

"Since long before I came to London."

He silently nodded. The poor man. He must be so very distraught. After all, to have one's love unreturned and a marriage proposal rejected would be dreadful.

Yet, did his stance straighten? Why did he appear more confused than upset?

"Mr. Hawkins, I am truly sorry if I have ever done

anything to lead you to believe that I might love you more than as my friend."

His eyes narrowed. "So, to be perfectly clear, you do not love me?"

"I am sorry. No."

"Then why did my mother, and yours, say that you did? Is this not why you came to Cornwall? Because you feared I might not return your love?"

Her hand flew to her mouth to stifle the laughter escaping her lips. Leaving London for fear of Mr. Hawkins *not* proposing? What an idea! "Forgive me, but that is quite the opposite of why I fled." Her smile soon faded away, replaced with a disbelieving scowl. "My mother said I was in love with you?"

He nodded in earnest. "Yes."

She shook her head, her lips pressed tightly together. When would she ever stop being surprised by Mother's trickery? "My mother told me that your mother said that *you* loved *me*." She could see him attempting to work out her words as she continued, her mind whirling. "Indeed, I left for fear of her urging me to accept your proposal because a rejection might hurt you."

His jaw twitched, realization lighting in his eyes. "My mother. Will she ever stop her meddling?" He sighed heavily. "Miss Summerfield, you must forgive me. For all of this."

A weight began to lift from around her shoulders, a warm sensation kindling in her chest. Before she could allow herself to hope, however, she pulled back. "Mr. Hawkins, do you love me?"

A light smile stretched across his lips. "No, I do not."

Her mouth parted with a sigh of relief before she shook her head. "Then why on earth are you here, proposing?"

With a sigh, Mr. Hawkins adjusted his cravat, looking very much as if he wished to remove the tight fabric from around his neck. "As I said, I was told your departure from London was evidence that you wished to marry me. Our mothers said that all of London believed an understanding existed between us, and if I did not follow you, your reputation would be ruined. Not to mention, both of our mothers would skin me alive."

He sighed, reaching for her hand and kissing the back of her fingers. The familiar confidence and kindness she had always associated with Mr. Hawkins returned, as did the color in his cheeks. "Miss Summerfield, I enjoy your company immensely. You were my one friend in London whose mind was filled with more than what to wear to the next ball and how to style your hair in the latest fashion. However, I cannot tell you how very relieved I am—please, do not be offended—that you are not in love with me."

Hannah laughed, relief washing over her. "Mr. Hawkins, I am so pleased to hear you say that! Oh, what a mess our mothers have made for us."

"Yes, and I will return straightaway to tell them what their interfering has done. Perhaps I ought to force them to inform all of London about their meddlesome actions. I fear their mouths have run away with them since my departure. I sincerely apologize if this does taint your reputation."

"Oh," she said, brushing aside his words with a wave of her hand, "worry not. That does not matter to me. Not out here, at any rate. But what of yours?"

He shrugged, appearing thoughtful. "Perhaps this is just the sort of thing that needed to happen for me to finally leave London behind. You know, I never cared for it. We have that in common, at the very least." He smiled. "Well, I am certainly happy this has all been resolved for the better."

Hannah dipped her head down, frowning. "I fear not everything has been resolved. Thomas—Mr. Causey, I believe he might suspect you and I are engaged."

"Oh, that is not right," Mr. Hawkins said, frowning. "No. Shall I speak with him? Tell him the truth of the matter?"

"That is very kind of you," she said, "but I must speak with him myself."

"Of course," he said with a quick nod. "I shall not keep you a moment longer then. I will leave for London as soon as I can."

He turned on his heel and made to return upstairs before she called after him. "Oh, Mr. Hawkins?" He paused on the first step. "I was meaning to ask, was my mother so very upset with my departure?"

"She was worried, yes. She sent for me the moment she discovered your absence, asking me to ride after you. I believe she knew, though, that your determination would see you arrive in Cornwall safely."

Hannah bit her lip. "Will you wait just one moment for me?"

He quirked a curious brow but nodded, and Hannah darted from the room to the nearby study.

Quickly, she scribbled out a note.

Mother,

Please forgive me for leaving Town without speaking to you first. I know you wished me to marry Mr. Hawkins, but I do not love him. I did not have the opportunity to forge a relationship with Father before he died, but I still long for one with you. I hope my actions do not damage our chance. Just as I hope the deceit you have used to keep me in London does not destroy the future I have chosen for myself. I pray we may forgive each other.

I can only trust now that you wish for my happiness. If you do, Mother, please know that I am happy, as I always have been in Cornwall. And I always will be. I am happy here amidst the wildflowers and moors, near the sea and the cliffsides.

And I am happy here with those I love. I hope you will one day understand.

With all my love,
Hannah

Quickly, she folded, sealed, and addressed the letter to her mother before returning to Mr. Hawkins.

"Please, will you give this to my mother?" she asked. "And, if you are to tell her about what has occurred, would you mind so very much leaving out any mention of Mr. Causey? She may not react favorably to his name, and I should like to see her reaction in person."

With an amused grin, Mr. Hawkins accepted the letter and tucked it into his jacket. "It would be my pleasure, Miss Summerfield." And he tipped his head to her before making his way upstairs.

As he departed, a sudden urgency welled up within Hannah to find Thomas and explain. Gone was the constrained woman from before, her worries dissipating and mind clearing.

Darting through the doorway, she left the manor behind, hardly noticing the rumbling thunder in the distance and the falling rain speckling her dress as she ran across the fields in the direction of Leighton House.

CHAPTER ELEVEN

The gray waves crashed upon the shore and rushed toward Thomas, who stood just out of the reach of the water frothing white on the darkened sand. He hardly noticed his shirt soaked through with rain, too preoccupied was he with his thoughts.

After all, it was his fault he and Hannah would never be together. He could have done something—*anything* when she was in London. Urged her to return to Cornwall, expressed his love to her in writing, even gone after her himself. He *had* feared rejection when her letters had stopped, but he should have realized her mother was behind it. Even knowing as much then, however, did not stop the ache within his heart.

Raindrops ran down his skin, and the bitter wind whistled in his ears. The cold air of the storm numbed his senses, and he welcomed it.

"Thomas?"

He held his breath. Had he imagined her voice above the sound of the roaring sea? He must have. She would no doubt be eating breakfast with her betrothed.

If only to rid himself of the dreadful image of Hannah laughing and smiling with the man she truly loved, Thomas turned around. His heart skipped a beat when he saw the woman walking toward him. Her hair was plastered against the sides of her face, her pink dress dripping wet, but she smiled, her dimples deep.

He narrowed his eyes. Why did she appear so happy?

"What are you doing here, Hannah?" he asked.

She stopped a few paces away from him. "I was on my way to Leighton House when I remembered how you enjoyed the sea during a storm. So I came here first, hoping to find you."

His throat constricted, making it hard for him to swallow. Hannah knew him as well as he knew her. But what was it all for if they were not to be together?

"You must be cold," he said, noting her lack of gloves, bonnet, and covering.

A sheepish grin graced her pink lips. "Yes, I left rather hastily."

He ran his fingers through his hair, water falling to his brow. "Why are you not with Mr. Hawkins?"

She took a step toward him. "Because he has returned to London to issue a rather stern reprimand to our mothers."

Thomas frowned. Their mothers? What did she mean? "Are you not to return with him then?"

She shook her head, and a spark of hope ignited in his heart.

"Why?" he asked.

A slow smile spread across her lips, and a frenzy arose within Thomas at the sight, his chest billowing with unrestrained hope. He rushed toward her, grasping her upper arms and staring down into her wide, blue eyes.

"Why are you not going with him, Hannah?"

Hannah stared up at Thomas, blinking away the drops that fell upon her lashes. The fear, the hope in his eyes, caused her breath to catch in her throat.

"Because," she began, smiling once more, "he does not love me, and I love someone else."

His brow softened, lines near his eyes crinkling as a smile crossed his lips. "Do you?"

She nodded. "In London, I was but a mere shadow of myself. The only thing keeping me from floating away forever was the small thread that tethered me to Cornwall, and to you. I could not be who I really was amidst the fine dances and the parties I attended. I could not be whole, for I had left behind a part of myself in Cornwall. My heart, with you."

She drew in a trembling breath, the love she had for him overpowering every thought.

He closed the distance between them, softly resting his forehead upon her own. She closed her eyes, feeling the warmth of his person as the rain dripped from his hair to slide down her temples.

His hands slipped around her face, her heart thumping against her chest as his thumb wiped away the rain and tears from her cheek. "You have been my dearest friend, Hannah, since we met upon this very beach as children. My feelings for you have only strengthened over the years, growing into a deep and lasting love. I can only hope that our childhood was merely the beginning of our lives together. That there will be many more races for me to win upon Tregalwen."

She laughed, shaking her head at his teasing. He joined in with laughter of his own before sobering once more. "Will you marry me, my love? So our memories together along these shores might never end?"

Hannah could not contain her smile. "Of course I will marry you, Thomas."

His lips found hers at once, firm yet gentle, and Hannah's knees trembled. The wind and rain swirled around them, the waves pounded upon the sand, but she focused entirely on Thomas and the love they shared. She never thought she could be so happy or feel such peace again. But as Thomas held her in his arms, she knew she was where she belonged.

She pulled back for a moment, staring up at him with twinkling eyes. "You may rest assured, though, when we have children of our own, I will raise them to be splendid riders, just so they may beat you in a race and teach you a little humility."

His deep laughter created a lightness within her she prayed would remain forever. "I would expect no less from you, Hannah." He wrapped his arms around her. "Just so long as you do not raise them to torment our servants, as well."

She laughed, locking her hands at the back of his neck as she pulled him in for another kiss. He responded with a sigh deep within his chest.

Hannah had thought she could not love the man any more than she did, but as each moment passed by, her love, born from years of waiting, of longing, expanded in her soul.

And she knew, with joy sailing throughout her body as powerful as the waves of the sea, that their love would last. For theirs was a love that could not be weakened by time nor distance. Theirs was a love that would remain strong forever.

Theirs was a love that was true.

THE END

AUTHOR'S NOTE

I hope you enjoyed this novella! If you couldn't tell from reading it, I am absolutely obsessed with Cornwall. I had the opportunity to visit the beautiful county a couple years ago, and I'm planning my next trip there soon. The rugged countryside, the craggy cliffs, and the views of the ocean are stunning. It has truly become my home away from home.

Writing this novella has helped ease my longing to return, until I can make it there again in person. As such, I am thrilled to have shared this novella with you, a prequel to my new *Cornish Romance* series. I can't wait to have you read the rest of the novels soon!

If you enjoyed this novella and want to receive the latest news about my future novels, sign up for my newsletter! I always share new and discounted clean romance novels, as well as fun polls, quotes, and giveaways. My newsletter subscribers are also the first to see sneak peeks and cover reveals!

Make sure to follow me on Facebook (for more clean romance deals) and Instagram (for photos of my travels to the UK and more)!

I hope to connect with you soon!

Happy reading,

Deborah

ABOUT THE AUTHOR

Deborah M. Hathaway graduated from Utah State University with a BA in English, Creative Writing. As a young girl, she devoured Jane Austen's novels while watching and re-watching every adaptation of Pride & Prejudice she could, entirely captured by all things Regency and romance.

Throughout her early life, she wrote many short stories, poems, and essays, but it was not until after her marriage that she was finally able to complete her first romance novel, attributing the completion to her courtship with, and love of, her charming, English husband. Deborah finds her inspiration for her novels in her everyday experiences with her husband and children and during her travels to the United Kingdom, where she draws on the beauty of the country in such places as Ireland, Yorkshire, and her beloved Cornwall.

Made in the USA
Columbia, SC
29 January 2024